WHAT WE SEE WHILE WE'RE FALLING

MEGAN DANG

To Katelyn, who listens to all of my stories

1

Mom always used to take me to see the stars when I was younger.

Stargazing was her favorite thing to do in the world. She and I would walk to the park next to my neighborhood and trek up the big grassy hill in the middle of the night. I remember how tired I was with my short legs and tiny strides, struggling to keep up with her.

"Why do we have to go up the hill?" I asked her.

"You can't see the stars from low ground," Mom told me. "They're much brighter when you see them from up high."

I couldn't find it in myself to care about a bunch of stupid stars. Not when my legs were aching with each step I took. I made it about halfway up the hill before stopping.

Mom walked a couple more steps before she realized I wasn't following her. She backtracked over to my side. "What's wrong?"

"My legs hurt," I complained.

Mom clicked her tongue, shaking her head. "Well, that's not going to work," she said. "You've still got a lot of stars to see, Drew."

Bending down, she scooped me up in her arms. She put me over her back and I clung onto her neck while she walked the rest of the way up the hill. I loved clinging to her like that. She was warm and safe and soft. When I was on top of her back, there was no space between myself and the sky, and I swear to god I was invincible.

We made it to the top of the hill, but Mom didn't set me down. She let me look up at the sky from her shoulders, which felt like the highest seat in the universe.

My breath hitched in wonder as I stared up at all of the stars. There were so many that I couldn't possibly even begin to count them. For every ten, every hundred, every thousand stars, I could count another infinite.

2

They were everywhere and never ending, peppered across the sky, twinkling down at me like they were smiling.

Mom was twinkling too. "Do you like them?" she murmured.

I couldn't even figure out how to form coherent words. My mouth was stuck open, my eyes as big as saucers.

One star darted across the sky, surging past the others. "That one's moving!" I exclaimed, pointing to it.

Mom looked too. "You're right," she said. "That's a shooting star."

Below me, Mom shook her head. "It's a *falling* star," she corrected me.

I looked down at her, frowning. "What do you mean?"

"Shooting star is a term we use for meteorites," Mom explained. "We say that because they look like they're shooting across the sky."

My eyes were glued to the glowing dot in the black night. It looked almost like a jet, streaking past the horizon. "But it *is* shooting across the sky."

"Not shooting," Mom said. "Falling. They're actually falling through space, then dying out when they hit the atmosphere."

"Falling stars," I repeated.

Mom hummed in agreement. I clung to her a little closer.

That night when I went to sleep, I imagined a thousand stars on my bedroom ceiling. All burning bright. All twinkling.

All falling, down and down towards the earth.

2

Going into sophomore year, I wasn't particularly excited to be back at school.

It wasn't as if my summer schedule had been enthralling even in the slightest. I spent most of the break playing video games and watching movies at Brent's house. Sometimes we went to Wallace's house, but a good 90% of the DVDs he owned were cheesy rom-coms and chick flicks. *Movies for middle school girls,* Brent would say, to which Wallace would turn pink and protest that they were his mom's DVDs.

I suppose I wasn't much better, with only a couple of banged-up 90's movies in my collection. It didn't really matter, though; we never hung out at my place. In fact, Wallace had never even seen my house before. Brent, who I'd known since kindergarten, used to come over to my house all the time until it happened. Wallace became our friend in eighth grade, after Mom was gone and my house became suddenly taboo.

It wasn't like I'd told Brent he couldn't come over anymore. I didn't tell him anything, really. He sort of just made up his own rules for me, the way everyone else did when this sort of thing happened. I'd picked up on those silent, unspoken rules over the years.

1. Don't talk about it.
2. Don't think about it.
3. Pretend it didn't happen.

The rules were surprisingly enticing, though simple, and I found that I adhered to them just the same as everyone else. They were easy to comprehend and even easier to follow.

So Wallace never asked about my house or about either of my parents. That'd be against the rules, obviously. It was kind of strange. I didn't even ask to not talk about the incident. People just naturally swerved around the topic as a whole on my behalf.

Movies, video games, TV— they were all easy too. Wallace, Brent and I had fun together doing sort of mindless activities like that. They didn't require us to have any deep or thoughtful conversations; they didn't require much thinking at all, really. It was just the three of us together, happy in the easiest way. So despite my summer being sluggish and repetitive, I was perfectly content with what I had.

Brent was the polar opposite of me. He was thrilled.

"I'm getting the team jackets this year," he told me excitedly. Whenever he got eager about stuff like this, he talked so quickly that my brain had to do extra work to keep up with him. "I customized them last night. Wanna see?"

I didn't even have time to respond before he practically flung his phone into my face. My eyes focused on the picture displayed on his dim screen. They were pretty simple jackets, dark blue with white sleeves and the word 'Mathletes' printed neatly across the breast pocket. I did find it kind of funny how they were designed like varsity jackets, as if Mathletes was an actual sport and not just Brent's tiny club. But that was how Brent saw Mathletes, after all— like a competitive sport. I still caught him polishing our first place tournament trophy from freshman year in his bedroom sometimes.

"Cool, right?" Brent said. He was grinning. "I already showed Wallace and he loves them."

I was dubious at first. "You're gonna order us *jackets?* Isn't that kind of a waste of money? There are only four of us."

The fourth, in addition to Brent, Wallace, and I, was Jessica Seymour— a girl who'd been on the Mathletes team ever since we assembled it in freshman year, and yet who Brent had only begun to fancy the day she started to wear lipstick this year. She was pretty— there was no denying that— and she was friendly, too. Of course, she wasn't quite friendly enough to hang out with us much outside of Mathletes practice, but it wasn't like we expected her to. It didn't matter. Brent was completely whipped for her, despite his crush being fairly new.

"That means I only have to pay for four jackets, Einstein." Brent pulled his phone back, pocketing it. "Anyway, don't worry about it. It's not like it's your money."

I looked up now, my eyes going wide. "Wait, what? You're gonna pay for all of them?"

"Yeah," he replied with a shrug. "It's not a big deal."

Impressed, I tried not to stare at him in awe. It was kind of hard to believe how willingly he was paying for all of us, but then I reminded myself that Brent was somewhat of an unstoppable force when he made up his mind. He was insanely stubborn by nature, but this also made him insanely passionate by nature, so he practically devoted his very being to Mathletes.

After school, we hung up Mathletes posters around the campus. Ever since freshman year, we'd been trying to draw in more students to the club, trying to get people to join the team. But judging by our practically nonexistent turnout, I had begun to speculate that there were just too many things about Mathletes that were unappealing for the average Eldridge student.

For one thing, Mathletes was a very small, exclusive group. The four of us were definitely the best math students in our grade, but it wasn't like Eldridge was an incredibly huge school to begin with.

Aside from that, Mathletes was a student-organized club, meaning it wasn't organized at all, really. With Brent being the president and founder of the club, he coordinated all of our practices and matches by himself. And he was kind of in love with Mathletes. If there was one thing Brent liked more than Jess, it was Mathletes. Luckily for him, the two were concentrated in the same place. And there was also the fact that Mathletes required a pretty good amount of dedication. We had practices every week after school and started tournaments about midway through the school year.

"I still can't believe we didn't have a single person try out for the team last year," Wallace said. He was struggling with a banner that was a good two feet taller than he was.

Jess frowned. "*I* tried out for the team last year," she said. She finished taping a flyer to a wall.

"Yeah, but aside from you, there's been no one else." Wallace paused. "Drew, can you get the other side…?"

"Four people is the minimum amount of members you can have on your team," I said as I helped Wallace unfold the banner. "If one of us calls in sick or quits, we're screwed."

"First of all, none of us are *quitting,* so there's no need to stress about that," Brent

11

told us. "Second, we're gonna get new members this year, okay? Don't worry. People just need to realize how cool Mathletes is."

"Or maybe they're just aware that it's not very cool at all," Jess snickered.

Wallace and I taped down the banner. We stepped back. Brent was standing and observing, squinting at it thoughtfully.

"Drew, your side needs to be higher," he said finally.

I blinked, looking back at it. The banner seemed pretty straight to me. "Really?"

"Yeah, I'm sure." Brent crossed his arms. "It's not even."

I hesitated for only a moment before going back to fix it. Behind me, Wallace said, "How can you even tell?"

"I just can," Brent said simply. "It has to be perfect."

"We're putting in a lot of work for this," Jess remarked. "It's gonna be really disappointing if we don't get any new recruits."

"We will," Brent promised. "Just wait and see."

Then he bent down and picked up our other banner. He unfolded it. It had to be at least seven feet long, making him look kind of tiny in comparison. He draped it over his shoulders and took off sprinting down the hallway.

We all picked up the remaining posters and followed after him. "What are you doing?" Wallace called between bouts of giggles.

"Mathletes is the coolest!" Brent yelled, his voice echoing through the empty hallway. The banner trailed after him as he ran, flowing elegantly in the wind. He looked like Superman with a Mathletes advertisement over his back in lieu of a cape.

Jess was laughing hysterically now, watching him tear down the hallway. Then she looked at me, grinning. "How many times do you think he's gonna have to say that until it comes true?"

3

The first few weeks of school passed by quickly and uneventfully. I had come to the ready conclusion that nothing would be different this year, and the months that followed would be just as monotonous as ever.

So when I bumped shoulders with a girl in the cafeteria line one day and mumbled a passive apology, I hadn't been expecting her to whirl all the way around and make full-on eye contact with me, right there in the middle of the crowded lunchroom.

For a second we held eye contact like that, just staring at each other. Confusion washed over me like a wave. Why was she looking at me like that? Maybe she hadn't heard me. So I tried again—

"Sorry," I said, a bit louder.

I offered up a polite smile, which she met with sharp dark eyes and none of her own to mirror it. When she still stared, I broke eye contact, too scared to hold it a moment longer.

But then she was talking, and so casually that I almost didn't realize she was talking to me at first. "You know, I think those are the scum of the earth."

I blinked dumbly. "Huh?"

She reached over to my lunch tray, tapping a finger against the plastic rim of the packaged fruit cup I'd picked up in line. "These things," she said. "Have you ever opened one of them before?"

I didn't know how to respond. "Yes?" I replied cautiously, unsure of whether I'd given her the answer she was waiting for.

"The juice spills everywhere. Makes the entire thing an abomination, if you ask me." She pursed her lips. "Besides, if you actually read the ingredients, it's hardly even fruit in there. Just a mesh of preservatives and artificial coloring."

"Everything has preservatives."

16

"Yeah, but *fruit* preservatives... those are the worst. Why ruin something that already tastes good naturally, you know? There's just no point."

I eyed her lunch tray. "So that's a better alternative?" Instead of a plastic fruit cup, a container of chocolate pudding sat innocently on her own tray.

"Exactly," she said without missing a beat. "It has more calories, which might warrant a hazard for anyone who should be watching their weight, but you could use a few extra pounds— here."

The girl grabbed my fruit cup right off my tray and swiped it out with pudding. I was too stunned to move. She looked back up at me with a look of satisfaction.

"That should do the trick," she said.

I stared after the girl as she picked up her tray and walked away. My head was spinning. I'd never so much as had a conversation with strangers in the lunch line, and yet here this girl was, criticizing my choices and swapping items out for me on my tray. Did that really just happen? Strange.

I made my way over to my lunch table and sat down next to Brent. As I picked up my sandwich, I realized that he and Wallace were dead silent. I looked up to see the two of them staring at me as if I'd grown a third arm.

I glanced cautiously behind me. There was nothing unusual— just the typical bustling of students. Meaning they were staring at *me*, and nothing else. I looked back at them.

"Um," I said. "What's up?"

"You talked to her," Brent hissed under his breath, as if he was scared she would somehow hear from the other corner of the lunch room she'd retreated to. "Oh my god, you talked to her."

"That girl?" I asked, pointing loosely in her direction. Brent and Wallace nodded vigorously in unison. "Who is she?"

"You haven't heard about her?" Wallace squeaked incredulously. "That's *Polly Park.*"

When he said her name, his voice dropped two octaves and became barely above a whisper. He said it like he was almost scared of it; he might as well have said *She Who Must Not Be Named.* "She's, like, all anyone's been talking about today."

I pressed my lips into a firm line, thinking hard for a moment. "No," I said decidedly, "didn't hear anything."

"She's a psychopath," Brent announced matter-of-factly.

"She's amazing!" Wallace exclaimed at the exact same moment.

I looked skeptically back and forth between the two of them. They were both leaning forward in their seats eagerly. I hadn't seen them this excited over anything since we won the Mathletes tournament last year.

"Really. Polly Park?" I said. Her name sounded foreign on my tongue, but I found it rolled off quite pleasantly. "What's the big deal about her?"

"She moved here," Wallace rambled, "so today's her first day. She sat next to me in math today and she's a riot—"

"The things that come out of her mouth, Drew, you would not believe," Brent cut in. "Talking like a madman— just the most outrageous things. She told Sara that she had split ends."

"Matt was chewing gum during class," Wallace said with shining eyes, "and she turned around and she was like, 'you're either gonna have to spit that out or chew quieter 'cause I can't hear myself think when your teeth are going like that.'"

Brent had a haunted look on his face. He leaned a little closer to me, eyes darting nervously around the cafeteria.

"She told Mr. Harding that his fly was down," he whispered.

I lost it at that, giving in to snorting laughter. "Okay," I snickered. "Sure she did."

Brent's nostrils flared, eyes flashing. "You think I'm kidding?" he nearly screeched. "Drew, she told me I should roll up the cuffs of my jeans. You wanna know why?"

I was already growing tired of their stories, which were sounding more and more like fables by the second. But I decided to play along. "Why?" I asked innocently.

Brent fumed. "Because," he said, "my legs look like *string beans.*"

I held his gaze for a long moment, saying nothing. Finally I lowered my head so I could see under the table.

"I can see that," I said.

Brent was hysterical.

"Stop looking!" he cried. "Drew, were you even listening to anything I said?!"

"I was!" I defended myself. "It just— okay, I don't think she actually said that to you, alright? That's all."

"Didn't you just talk to her?" Wallace said. "What'd she say to you?"

Brent looked at me now, attention piqued. "Well," I said, "she bashed fruit cups and told me to eat pudding because I look like I could use extra calories…"

"See? She's weird!" Brent said.

"Yeah, she was a little weird," I admitted. "But she didn't come across as *psychopathic*." I paused for a second, glancing at Wallace. "Or amazing, for that matter."

Besides, she looked too *normal* to be anywhere near the sort of creature they were describing. In fact, she had one of the most forgettable faces I'd seen in a while. Already I was struggling to remember what she looked like. She had long black hair and dark eyes and hairy brows— almost incredibly mundane features. There was nothing striking about her.

"You'll see," Brent said. "Just wait, you'll see."

22

His eyes drifted past my head to the opposite side of the cafeteria. I glanced back, following his line of sight to where Polly was sitting and spooning pudding into her mouth.

I frowned. "Why do you keep looking at her?"

"Not at Polly," Wallace giggled. "He's looking at *Jess.*"

Brent hit Wallace on the arm. "Shut up!"

My eyes returned to Polly once more, and only this time did I see Jess seated next to her, howling with laughter. One thing that hadn't changed about Jess since the day I met her was that she was a complete glutton for gossip. Watching her nod along excitedly while Polly talked, I began to realize that it made perfect sense that the two of them would be fast friends. When I looked back at Brent I saw that his face had turned a bright, glowing shade of pink.

Wallace kept laughing. "You look like a tomato."

"Ha, ha, whatever." Brent pouted. "We'll see who's laughing when you're still single, Wallace."

"Wait, what?" Now Wallace's goofy grin melted away, replaced by an expression of curiosity. "You're gonna ask her out?"

Brent glanced at me. "Halloween," he said.

He'd conceived the Halloween idea as soon as school started, which was conveniently as soon as he'd developed his crush on Jess. I raised my eyebrows. "Just because she's going to your party doesn't mean she's going to be your girlfriend."

"Oh ye of little faith," Brent remarked. "Listen, I've got a plan, alright?"

I only half-believed him. But then again, that was where I found myself at a lot of the time lately. I didn't really think that he had a plan in line. I didn't really think that pudding was a better option than fruit cups. I *really* didn't think that Polly Park was a tornado that had arrived at our school to tear up life as we knew it, to uproot everything we believed in and destroy everything I thought I knew about myself.

But I didn't know for sure until when, three days later, she appeared in my English class.

4

From the beginning of the semester, the seat in the desk next to mine had been blissfully undisturbed. One day it was there, empty as always, so peacefully vacant. The next day, Polly was sitting inside of it— how perfectly she seemed to fit, too, with her legs sprawled out underneath the table in a way that made her long skirt ride up her waist a bit. She was leaning back all the way until the crown of her silky black hair touched the wall.

When she saw me, she didn't wave, or smile, or introduce herself. I wasn't sure why I'd expected her to do those things, anyway. I sat down in my seat next to her and she didn't even look in my direction. So naturally, when she started speaking, it took me a moment to realize she was actually talking to me.

"I was in CP English before, but they made me switch schedules so I could be in

Honors," she said. "This school district is ridiculous. I'd never even heard of CP and Honors classes until I came here."

Now she turned to look at me. Her eyes were small in size, but she was opening them wide, so she looked kind of like a deer. I noticed that her eyes were the darkest brown I'd ever seen— they didn't look brown at all, in fact. They looked black now that she was staring at me, black without a fleck of color.

"I used to go to school in Eagle River," she said. "That's in Wisconsin. It was way smaller than this campus. Anyway, we never had CP and Honors there." She raised her eyebrows. "I mean, aren't those just fancy words for *dumb* and *smart*?"

I snickered a little bit at this, in spite of myself. After a few seconds, I noticed with a jolt of fear that she wasn't laughing at all, her eyes dead serious.

"Um," I said, self-consciously swallowing back my bouts of laughter. "Welcome to smart English, then."

She sat back in her chair a little and glanced at her hands. Then back at me. "So," she said conversationally. "How was your pudding?"

I couldn't help it. I laughed again. Even though she still didn't laugh with me, I found myself unable to stifle it this time. There was just something so strange about the way she talked, open and unguarded and unbothered, really, by any sort of expectations that most people deemed normal for casual, polite banter. She disregarded all of the social cues that I worked so hard to perfect; she didn't seem to think before she spoke, she just talked and she just *was*, and it was impossible not to smile at the sheer weirdness of her demeanor.

"It was good," I said. "Thanks for the suggestion."

"I'm Polly Park." I liked how she said her first and last name like that, just laid it out plain and clear for me.

"Drew Hartford." My own name didn't roll off my tongue nearly as easily as hers did back when I said it in the cafeteria.

She held out her palm, which caught me off guard a little. Most people didn't shake hands. I thought that kind of formality was reserved for adults; I'd never voluntarily shaken hands with another high schooler before. But I reached out and I shook hers. Her hand was soft, but her grip was firm.

"Drew Hartford," she parroted back to me. On second thought, my name didn't sound so bad, at least not when she said it. "Oh, yes, I know about you, Drew. Wallace mentioned your name in class. Math genius, right?"

I balked a little. "I wouldn't say *that*..."

"And yet you're in smart English, too. So, what, then? You're just smart in everything?"

"Any fool can get into honors English. It's an easy class."

My intention was to sound humble, but I realized only after I said it how cocky it must have made me sound, seeing as she'd only just arrived in honors English herself. My eyes widened a bit in horror. "I meant to say—"

"Oh, no, I get it," Polly said. I tried to intervene once more but she silenced me with an elegant sweep of her hand. "Now I know that you are really good at English too, regardless of how you try and deny it. I'm glad you told me. It's just your honest opinion, after all."

"No, it's not," I tried to say. She just raised an eyebrow at me, calling my bluff. How did she know I was bluffing? So I amended, "Even if it's my opinion, I shouldn't have said it out loud."

She looked genuinely surprised, like that had never once occurred to her as a valid option. "Why?"

"Because it's mean."

Polly barked out a laugh. "You think that was *mean*? Oh, boy. You think I'm offended?"

She didn't even give me a chance to respond. She reached out and patted me on the head twice, like a dog.

I was shell-shocked, paralyzed, petrified. She didn't. She did *not* just pet me like a dog.

Except she did. And now she pulled her hand back, beaming up at me.

"You're cute," Polly said. "You know, Wallace told me you were a nice boy."

"Did— did you just pet me?" I asked faintly.

"Yes, it's all coming back to me now," Polly went on, ignoring me. "Wallace really talked highly of you. You're the smartest kid on the Mathletes team."

"There are only four of us."

"And you're the smartest," Polly said without missing a beat. She leaned over and poked me in the arm. "No need to lie about it."

I swallowed. "I didn't *lie* about anything."

"Yes, you did. You undersold yourself," she told me. "Here, I'll show you what I

31

mean. You know you're freakishly smart but you acted like, 'oh, no big deal, I'm okay at math, I guess.' Me, on the other hand, I can confidently say— without losing any seams of the truth— I am horrible at math."

I was smiling now, in spite of myself. "Okay, but now I'm thinking you're probably underselling yourself too."

"I'm not," she said matter-of-factly.

Then her eyes lit up. She unzipped her backpack, took out a folded piece of paper, placed it on my desk.

"I just got that math test back today," she told me casually.

I unfolded it and found myself face-to-face with a bright red D across the front of the page. My first instinct was to gawk, but I felt her eyes focusing intensely on my face, waiting for a reaction, so I tried to keep my expression neutral.

"That's— that's not so bad," I forced out.

Polly laughed. "You lied again," she sang.

"You didn't, um." I folded the paper back up and handed it to her. I was almost embarrassed, as if I was the one who flunked the test and not her. "You didn't have to show that to me."

"Well, I wanted you to know."

I gave her a funny look. "That you failed your test?"

She looked up at me with nothing funny in her own eyes. All business. "That I mean what I say."

"Mr. Hartford," Mrs. Pruitt called.

The two of us looked up. I felt every head in the classroom turn, every pair of eyes settling on me. That had to be the single most uncomfortable feeling in the world. I forced a polite smile onto my face.

"Yes?" I said mechanically.

"Care to tell the class what you were talking to Ms. Park so loudly about?"

Mrs. Pruitt wasn't malevolent. She didn't say it to be cruel or to humiliate me in front of the other students. That didn't keep my face from burning like I was on fire.

"Um," I started.

Then Polly suddenly swooped in. "I was the one talking," she announced to the class.

Everyone fell silent. I tried not to gape at her— she sat up straight in her seat with her shoulders back, looked every single student right in the eye, as if she was challenging them to respond. She knew nobody would. How could we? How could anyone possibly respond to a person like her? She was demanding, she was open, she was completely herself with absolutely nothing to hide.

And then, even though no one asked her to, she added: "I was showing Drew that I got a D on my math test."

I was grateful to be sitting at my desk, because if I'd been standing I would have gone completely weak at the knees. I stared at her in both awe and horror, not quite sure

I'd heard her actually say that out loud to the entire class.

The surprise on Mrs. Pruitt's face mirrored my own. She quickly regained her composure, though, clearing her throat. "Well, that's fine, Ms. Park," she said slowly. She looked amused, even though I could tell she was trying to hide it. "But you are in my class now, so I would appreciate if you discussed math after school."

"Sure," Polly said.

After the bell rang, I waited back a few moments for Polly to pack her things into her bag. When she looked up and saw me standing over her, she wrinkled her nose.

"Why are you hovering like that?" she asked.

I took a self-conscious step back, feeling like a creep, but she just started giggling. She slung her bag over her shoulder and we walked out of the classroom together.

"I can't believe you said that," I confessed to her as we walked.

Polly stuck her arms out to her sides. She looked like a bird with its wings spread out. As she walked, she twirled her arms around herself like she was flying. "What's so hard to believe?"

"You. I don't know. Just—" I paused, trying to let all of my jumbled thoughts sort themselves out in my brain. "Aren't you, like, embarrassed? At all?"

"You're funny," Polly said, stopping in her tracks and looking at me. She dropped her arms back down. I stopped walking too. "There are worse things in life than failing a math test, Drew Hartford."

"That doesn't mean you should go around announcing it in front of entire classrooms of people."

Polly paused for a moment. She pursed her lips. "I wasn't thinking about whether or not I'd be embarrassed saying it," she told me. "The reason I said it was because I didn't want Mrs. Pruitt to punish you for something

36

you didn't do. You were fully equipped to let her do that, weren't you?"

I didn't respond.

A smug look crossed her face. "That's what I thought. So how about a 'thank you', then?"

"Thank you," I said.

She looked skeptically at me, like she didn't believe me, so I added, "I mean it." Her expression softened a bit. "You're just, um...." I was trying to find the right words to describe her. Any word to describe her, really. Evidently, it wasn't working. It seemed like every adjective in my vocabulary had suddenly escaped my mind. "You're very... very..."

"Very very," she said, her lips quirking up in a smile.

My mouth felt dry. "Very very," I agreed numbly.

"Well, color me very very flattered," Polly cooed. She poked me in the arm. "I like you, Drew."

And with that, she turned and disappeared into the endless sea of students.

5

She liked me.

As I ate dinner with my dad that night, that was the only thing I could think about. The two of us sat together in complete silence, the only sounds filling the dining room the occasional scrape of our forks against our plates. But in my head Polly's voice was singing, her face was turning towards mine, she was reaching out and she was petting me like a dog—

You're cute. You're a nice boy.

Her hand was stroking my hair. Her black eyes seemed to be blue and green and brown and every single color *but* black. Nobody had ever touched me so openly like that without any seams of regret or embarrassment, except maybe Mom. Instead, I was the one feeling embarrassed, despite the fact that Polly was the one who initiated the action. She just did whatever she wanted whenever she wanted to.

Did you just pet me? I had asked her. And she didn't even acknowledge it.

"How was school?"

I looked up from my plate. Dad was staring at me from across the table. Our dining table was only a few feet long, but the distance between us felt immeasurable when I looked at him from the opposite side.

"Fine," I said shortly.

Dad set his fork down. "Anything new?"

Her.

I pressed my lips together, making it look like I was in deep thought before I shook my head. "No, nothing new," I lied instantly.

Except that...

She liked me.

Dad smiled at me a little. "You said that pretty quickly," he said with a chuckle.

Now I looked up too, half-amazed that he'd been able to observe that. He really had been paying attention to me.

"So you noticed," I said.

40

He did a full-on laugh now, and suddenly I found myself doing it too. We were laughing together at the dining table. When was the last time *that* had happened? My stomach fluttered a bit. It felt good.

"I did notice," he said. He looked at me then and I looked at him. "So what's new, then? What's on your mind?"

"Well," I started. "In my English class there's this—"

I was cut off by a loud, abrupt ringing. Dad winced as he pulled his cell phone from his pocket.

"Work," he said, glancing at me apologetically. "I've been waiting on this call all day, Drew, I—"

"It's fine," I told him. "Go ahead, take it. I don't mind. I was finished eating anyway."

Dad gave me a long look. He grimaced a bit, but he didn't make any comment about how quickly I'd responded this time. Instead he just swiped his thumb across his phone screen and held it up against his ear.

"Hello, Bill Hartford talking..."

I cleaned up the table while Dad spoke on the phone. After I was done, I left him downstairs, retreating to my bedroom.

I wasn't sure why I'd even thought about telling him about Polly. Or anything that was going on in my life, really. Now I just felt embarrassed for considering it. I decided it was just because of the moment, because of that feeling I got inside when we both laughed and for a second I felt like nothing had ever changed between us, like he was just my dad and I was just his kid and that was it.

But I reminded myself that wasn't how things were anymore. Dad had work, and I had myself. We were both doing fine that way.

Why would I tell him about Polly? Just because...

Just because she liked me?

Well, to be fair, the definition of 'like' was extremely ambiguous in the life of a high schooler. You could *like* sweet potato fries, but that didn't mean you would make out with them. Or maybe you would, just not in front of other people.

There was the kind of *like* that happened between friends; there was the kind of *like* that happened when two people went out together; there was the kind of *like* that happened when someone was maybe just pondering a relationship that was beyond a platonic one.

So which was it? Did she like me? Or did she *like*-like me? Or did she like-like-*like* me?

It had to be…

I like you, Drew.

My stomach felt very strange.

Polly, I thought to myself as I flopped face down onto my bed. *What have you done to me?*

6

She showed up to watch Mathletes practice.

It was unexpected, to say the least. We always held practices in the multi-purpose room, which was also where we held matches when our school hosted them.

Because he was president, Brent ran all of our practices. He wrote problems on a whiteboard, which Jess, Wallace, and I worked out as quickly as we could. Occasionally we alternated, but for the most part Brent made sure to separate himself as the leader. I think he always just liked being in charge of things. He was just wired that way.

I almost always buzzed in faster than Wallace and Jess. But every time Jess finished first, Brent would go, "Nice, Jess!" with the dumbest grin on his face, and I don't know why that kinda bothered me. It wasn't like I particularly wanted him to say that for me, or even for Wallace when either of us answered first. I was just annoyed by how fake-nice he was around her, always uncharacteristically chipper when she was nearby.

I'd just buzzed in on one of the first questions. Brent called out, "Drew?"

And I said, "Four rad six."

And he said, "Correct."

And Jess said, "Polly!"

We all looked out into the empty multi-purpose room seats. Except they weren't empty anymore— Polly was sitting in the front row.

She had her eyes glued to us on the stage. She had the most fascinated expression on her face, as if she were watching a theater play instead of a bunch of sophomores answering math problems in complete silence. She even clapped her hands for me, looking up from her seat, and I just watched her, too baffled to say anything.

"Hi," said Polly. Not to Jess. But not to me either. I don't know. When she said hi then, she didn't say it to any single person; it seemed like she said it to the entire world. "I'm just tuning in, don't mind me."

Jess was elated. Wallace looked amused. Brent, on the other hand, looked more peeved off than anything, but I could see him struggling to keep his expression pleasant.

See? There it was. Fake-nice.

"Okay," Brent forced out. "We're just gonna keep going then."

I was expecting Polly to be distracting, sitting there and spectating us from the front row, but she wasn't. She didn't say anything. She didn't clap after that, she just sat there and watched through the entire practice.

I buzzed first on every single question after she sat down. When we finished, Jess instantly jumped down from the stage and ran over to Polly.

"Hey!" Jess said. "You didn't have to come, you know. These things are always incredibly boring to watch."

"I liked watching," Polly told her.

Then a crooked grin spread across Jess's face. "*Sooo,*" she said. "Did you hear anything about Sara?"

"She was talking to her friends about it in chem today."

"And?"

Polly shrugged, nonchalant. "I overheard everything."

Jess's eyes sparkled. She opened her mouth to speak, but Brent cut her off.

"Drew won this match," he said. "Wallace, Jess, that means we have to review answers."

Jess sighed. She turned around and looked at me. "When *don't* you win the match?" she mused. Then she glanced back at Polly. "This will only take a minute." She climbed back onto the stage and regrouped with Wallace and Brent.

While I watched her separate from Polly, I accidentally made eye contact with Polly for a brief second. I tried to look away. I felt her gaze lingering on me, piercing and shocking. I used every ounce of my willpower to keep

47

my gaze focused on the back wall, but there was something about knowing she was watching me that drew me in and once it did I was a complete goner. I couldn't keep myself from looking back at her, standing alone at the foot of the stage.

She was still looking at me, as I suspected. When our eyes met once more, Polly lifted a finger and made a playful little *'come here'* motion. And once more I found myself obeying, stepping down from the stage and stopping in front of her.

"Why'd you come here?" I asked her, trying my best to sound casual. I slipped my hands into my coat pockets. I was attempting to mask how nervous I was— of course I was nervous around her, she was Polly Park and there had never been anyone or anything quite like her before, and I doubted there ever would be— but part of me worried she could read the lie all over my face.

But that was the difference between me and her, I guessed. When Polly talked, all of

48

her emotions were on full display on her face. Me, on the other hand, I'd become pretty good at hiding when I wanted to.

"Jess told me to," she said.

"Oh." She started giggling. I frowned at her.

"What?" I said.

"You," she said, "you're funny." Then she imitated my voice: "*Oh.*" More snickering. "Why do you sound so disappointed? Were you hoping I'd say I came to see you?"

My face felt warm. Distantly, I wondered how it could be this hot in an empty air-conditioned room in the middle of October.

"No," I said way too quickly. "I mean, yeah. I mean, I— I don't..."

Polly studied my face, amused. "Would you believe me if I told you that, Drew Hartford?"

I thought for a moment. She was doing that thing again— asking me impossible questions, making me overanalyze every possible answer.

I made up my mind.

"Yes," I said slowly. "I would."

A smile lit up her face. Her eyes twinkled. She hadn't been expecting that answer, but I knew she liked it.

"Yeah?" she said. "Why?"

"Because you mean what you say."

Polly had a strange look on her face, an expression I couldn't quite place.

"That's right," she said. She reached out and tapped my arm with a little paper pamphlet she was holding. "Well, you would be correct."

It was only then that I realized she actually *was* holding a little paper pamphlet. I peered down at it. "What's that?"

Polly glanced down at her hand. "Some poem called *The Second Coming*. It's pretty edgy. Here, I'll read it for you." She cleared her throat theatrically, holding the paper out in front herself. "'Turning and turning in the widening gyre—'"

"'The falcon cannot hear the falconer'," I said.

Polly stopped and looked up, her dark eyes huge in surprise. "You know this?"

"It's famous. William Yeats. I've read plenty of his work before."

"For class?"

I shrugged. "For fun." I was trying to sound casual.

Polly grinned anyway. "Oh boy," she said. "You're a real freak, aren't you? You read poetry for fun?"

"I—" I paused. Worried at my lip for a second. I decided to ignore that. "Well, what are you reading it for?"

"Literature Society," she told me. "Which you should join, by the way."

I frowned. "Isn't that Mrs. Pruitt's club?" I asked. Polly nodded. "Yeah, I don't think she's real fond of me."

It was Polly's turn to frown. "What makes you say that?"

51

"I just get the feeling that she thinks I don't care about literature, since I'm so focused on math."

"Do you?"

"Do I what?"

"Care about literature."

I swallowed. "Well, yeah. A little."

"I think you care—" Polly poked me in the arm— "a *lot.*"

I looked at her kind of sideways. "What makes you say that?" I said, mocking her tone.

"Well, Mr. *Smart English,*" Polly said, and, yeah. She was better at the whole mocking thing than I was. "Aside from the fact that you apparently read poetry for fun, I get the feeling you try hard in everything you do. And this wouldn't be an exception." She tilted her head at me. "True?"

"I guess, but I'm, you know." I gestured awkwardly around myself. "I'm in Mathletes."

"What's that got to do with anything?"

"It means that I should be focusing on math." I found that it wasn't really my voice talking at all then, but more of an agglomeration of the message that all of my friends and teachers had always told me collectively. "Math is what's going to get me into college, after all."

"That has got to be the *dumbest* logic I've ever heard," Polly marveled. I furrowed my brow at her, but I let her continue. "Okay, so you're good at math. Who cares? If you like English, then why can't you just do both?"

I knew she had a point. That didn't make me any less nervous. What was the point in pursuing English if I wasn't going to use it ever again in my life? As soon as I graduated from high school, I'd spend the rest of my life plugging numbers into equations and calculating integers. I was never going to have the time to touch a book cover. I was settled; I was fine.

I decided on a different counterargument. "I don't have time," I said half-heartedly.

Polly stared at me incredulously, like she couldn't believe I was really going for a last-ditch argument like this. Frankly, I couldn't either. She said, "How do you think I came to watch your practice, Drew? Luckily for you, Literature Society ends at 3:30, which is exactly when Mathletes practice begins. You could easily do both. Nice try, though."

"You're not going to give up on this, are you?" I asked. "You must've been really lonely there today."

"Yes, I'm so pathetically *lonely*," Polly sighed dramatically. Then she reached her hand out, pressed a paper pamphlet into my own hand. "I took two on accident, so you can have this one."

I glanced down at it. *The Second Coming.* "Do I have to annotate this?"

"Only if you want to."

Onstage, Brent, Jess, and Wallace had finished reviewing their problems. Jess hurriedly leapt back down and linked her arm through Polly's.

"Okay," Jess said eagerly. "Let's go."

Polly's eyes rolled up to meet mine. "I'll see you at Literature Society next month," she told me, practically singing.

"Okay," I heard myself say.

I really never had a choice to begin with whenever I was around her.

Jess and Polly disappeared from the multi-purpose room, Jess laughing the entire way out. Brent stepped down from the stage too now, followed shortly by Wallace.

"What's she on about?" Brent demanded. He sounded irritated.

I blinked. "Some drama with Sara Dean?"

"Not to Jess," Brent said, "to you. *Literature* Society? What's that?" He leaned over and snatched the pamphlet from my hands. "Is this *poetry?*"

I took it back from him with a sigh. "It's just a stupid English club."

"And?"

I paused, hesitant. "And she wants me to go with her."

Brent raised his eyebrows. "Really. Since when did you like *English?*"

"Since his girlfriend liked it," Wallace snickered.

I ignored both of them. I gingerly folded up the pamphlet Polly had given me and put it inside my backpack.

"Wait," Brent said. He grabbed me by the shoulder and turned me around, kind of roughly. His eyes were wild. "You don't like her, do you?"

"No," I said, too quickly. *But she likes me.* Whatever that meant.

"Good," he said.

Now I frowned at him, suddenly on guard. "What's that supposed to mean?"

"What do you think?" he countered. "We talked about this, dude. She's psycho. You probably shouldn't be getting too close to someone like her, that's all I'm saying."

"She's not psycho."

"She's weird," Wallace said thoughtfully. I looked at him sharply and he added, "But that's not a bad thing."

"Well, it's not a good thing, either," Brent huffed. "Is she bullying you into going to literature club with her, Drew?"

"Maybe I'll go because I want to," I said.

Brent's jaw dropped. "Huh?"

"But we have practice," Wallace objected.

"So I can go to both. Their meetings end before practices start."

"You're crazy," he said, shaking his head. "You know, it's your life you're screwing with, okay? If you seriously want to waste your time, be my guest. Just don't miss practice. Okay?"

"Okay," I heard myself say.

Zero objections. Ever.

I stood and stared at my shoelaces while Brent walked out of the multi-purpose room. Saying nothing.

Wallace hung back a little longer, looking sympathetic. He offered up a smile.

"Bye, Drew," he said meekly.

There was a smile on my face too. But it didn't mean anything.

"Bye," I said back, hardly aware of it.

7

Halloween night. Brent had been texting me all day, as if I could forget it was tonight when it was the only thing he'd been talking about for weeks on end.

"Dad, I'm heading out," I called as I pulled on my coat.

Dad was in the kitchen, bent over his computer. He had his reading glasses on and was working feverishly. "Where are you going?" he said back absently.

"Brent's house." I laced up my shoes. "He's having a party."

Dad looked up now. His glasses were slightly askew; he didn't bother adjusting them. "Do you need me to drive you?"

"No, no, I'll walk. It's fine." I finished tying my shoes and stood up straight. "See you, Dad."

I was already closing the door as he said goodbye to me.

I found myself always trying to get out of his hair as soon as I possibly could. Dad had always been busy. Even though Dad worked at home, he worked full-time. Mom was the one who usually had more off days and free time to spend with me.

After she was gone, Dad sort of melted under the pressure.

We all have our own ways of coping. His was to refuse to talk about it and shut away the rest of the world.

He kept more to himself than ever now, closing himself off, becoming so distant that he became out of reach entirely. Work became his refuge, his safeplace. It gave him something else to think about.

I didn't want to interfere with that. I didn't want to interfere with any part of the routine he'd fallen into, really. I nodded along. I told him everything was fine. I walked myself places instead of asking him for rides.

I didn't have my driver's license yet. I had my permit. More accurately, I had my permit for a good few *months* now, but I hadn't been behind the driver's wheel of a car since my mom died.

Mom used to take me to parking lots all the time, convinced I should learn to drive as soon as possible. I'd only been eleven when she first stuck me into the driver's seat of her car. Dad always said it was way too early for me to start practicing, but Mom insisted that it was never too early.

"Once you get your license, you'll be thanking me," she used to say. "Everyone else will have to practice for half a year until they can pass their driver's test. You'll already be a pro— you'll be the first out of all your friends to get on the road."

Sometimes I thought Dad was right. I was far too young to be driving around, even in deserted parking lots. I was horrible at first. The entire car would waver back and forth whenever I tried to drive in a straight line.

But by the time I was thirteen, I was an expert. I'd become a master at everything—

turning, signaling, the whole shabang. I was even good at parallel parking. Like, who on earth is good at *that?*

That was three years ago.

And the last time I'd driven a car.

Now, the idea of sitting behind the driver's wheel of a car made me absolutely petrified. So I wasn't planning on doing it again anytime soon.

That was why I walked to Brent's house alone that night, despite his house being a good couple miles away. And that was also why I arrived at the party late.

And *that* was why, when I knocked on the door, Brent immediately opened up and then grabbed my arm, dragging me inside the house.

"Happy Halloween to you too," I said as Brent hauled me alongside him. Wallace was there too, trailing after us with wide, nervous eyes.

"You're *late*," Brent said, jabbing a finger in my face.

"By fifteen minutes," I said back. "What'd I miss?"

Brent grabbed my shoulders and turned me toward the living room. "That."

The living room was bustling with other kids, but somehow Polly was the first person I saw. Scratch that— there was *definitely* a reason why she was the first person I saw, and it was the bright yellow striped skirt she was wearing over black stockings. Only a handful of people had shown up wearing costumes, but even so, none of them were nearly as over the top as hers. She completed the look with a pair of shimmery fabric wings and two pom-poms that bounced over her head as antennae.

My eyes drifted to the side, where Jess was standing next to her. Jess wasn't in costume, but she'd gotten even more dolled up than usual, curled her hair and wore a black dress and everything.

"Pretty," I commented half-heartedly.

"He hasn't talked to her since she got here," Wallace informed me.

I whipped my head around to look at Brent, furrowing my brow. "What?"

Brent huffed, exasperated. "I'm getting there, okay? Listen, do you think you could, like… you know… make your way over there, maybe talk with her a bit about me, or?"

I shot him a look. "I thought you said you had a plan."

"This— this is part of the plan!" Brent spluttered, his ears bright pink. "Just, okay, Drew, you need to do this for me. Please."

"What about Wallace?" I asked. "Why didn't you have Wallace help you?"

Wallace boggled at the mere mention of his name. He gave me a frantic look, like *please don't bring me into this.*

Brent easily deflected my suggestion anyway. "You're tight with Polly, aren't you?" I didn't respond to that. "So it's more natural for you to talk to them."

64

It seemed awfully convenient that Brent criticized me for talking to Polly, but was suddenly interested in having me do it tonight, when he was getting something out of it. "What do you even want me to ask her?" I asked, exasperated.

"Just talk to her about what a great party this is, maybe talk me up a little..." Brent twiddled his thumbs nervously. "And then say I think her dress is cute."

"You want me to be your *messenger?*" I said in disbelief. "What is this, middle school?"

Brent clicked his tongue, shaking his head. "It's called flirting, Drew. You wouldn't understand."

"I don't get why you can't just tell her that yourself."

"Aloofness, Drew, aloofness." Brent grabbed me by the shoulders and spun me around forcefully before giving me a shove in Jess's direction. "Now go."

I sighed, but I found myself obeying anyway. I walked over to the living room where Jess and Polly were standing. The two of them watched me approach.

"Hi, Drew," Jess said.

"What are you supposed to be?" Polly said.

"I'm not wearing a costume."

"Boring." Polly stood a little straighter, spun around for me to see her fabric wingspan, then back around for me to see her yellow and black striped skirt twirl around her legs. Her antennae bobbed up and down over her head. "I'm a bumble bee."

"I couldn't tell."

"Fun party," said Jess.

"Yeah," I agreed. "Brent's pretty cool for organizing this whole thing, huh?"

Jess laughed a little. She seemed kind of confused. "I guess?"

"Speaking of Brent." Real smooth. I fought back the urge to sigh again. "He thinks your dress is really cute."

Now Jess's expression shifted. It must've clicked with her just what I was trying to do.

Her eyes glimmered playfully. "Really?" she said. Yup, she was definitely in on the game too, now.

"Really."

"Brent said that?"

"Yup."

She glanced over my shoulder at Brent, then looked back at me. "Tell him I think he looks pretty handsome himself," she said, batting her eyelashes. She laughed some more.

I smiled uneasily before turning and walking back over to Brent and Wallace. Brent was anxiously tapping his fingers against the rim of his cup, eyes wide as he watched me draw closer. "What'd she say?!" he demanded.

"She thinks you look handsome."

Wallace fake gagged behind Brent. Brent elbowed him and then looked back at me wildly. "Tell her to try some of the punch."

I made a face. "Brent," I complained.

"Drew!" he complained back at me. "Come on, man, just do it! She's never gonna come over here otherwise."

I sucked in a breath between clenched teeth, but once more I found myself obeying him. I walked back over even though I felt like the biggest idiot in the universe.

Jess was already waiting for me, twirling a strand of hair around her fingers. Anticipating the next message. She smiled when she saw me.

"Hi," she said again in a singsong voice.

"Hi," I said wearily. I ran a tired hand through my hair. "He, uh—"

"Drew, d'you know where the bathroom is?" Polly asked.

I blinked, straightening. "Yeah," I said.

"Show me."

"Okay," I said dumbly. "Uh, okay. Follow me."

"Be right back," Polly told Jess.

Polly and I ducked past the crowd as I led her to the bathroom. Once we arrived in front of the bathroom door, Polly turned around until she was facing me.

Then she jabbed me sharply in the shoulder with her finger.

I recoiled, wincing. "Ow!"

"I just stung you," she said.

I rubbed my shoulder irritably. "Okay…?"

"You wanna know why?"

I gave her a look. "Not particularly."

"Ha, ha. It's because you're being a tool, Drew Hartford. But you realize that, don't you?"

"A tool," I echoed.

"Exactly," Polly said. "As in, Brent and Jess are using you to flirt with each other and you're just letting them."

I shrugged. "Yeah."

"And that doesn't bother you?"

I shrugged again. Polly rolled her eyes.

"It bothers you," she said, "but you'd never say that out loud, huh? You're kinda dumb, you know that?"

"Yeah."

Polly snorted. "Come here," she said, grabbing my arm and tugging me along.

"I thought you needed to go to the bathroom," I said as she led me out the front door of Brent's house.

"False," she said. "I asked you to show me where the bathroom was. You did. And now we're leaving."

"Where are we going, exactly?"

"It's Halloween," Polly called as we stepped out onto the porch. "Take a wild guess."

Brent's neighborhood was big. That didn't intimidate Polly one bit.

"We're gonna get through the entire place," she chanted confidently at me. "Got it?"

"I'm not even wearing a costume," I protested.

"Yes, you are." She patted me on the shoulder. "Confused math genius nice boy with more to him than meets the eye."

I glanced up at her. "You think there's more to me than meets the eye?"

"I observe people," she said shortly.

"So you've observed me."

"Correct."

"What do you see?"

"It's not quite about what *I* see," she told me, tapping her chin thoughtfully. "More about what other people see. Tell me, Drew, what does everyone think about you? When you walk down the hall, what does everyone see?"

"Um…" I thought for a second. "Math genius."

"Is that true?"

I thought again. "I guess."

"Okay, what else?"

"A nice boy…"

"True?"

"I guess." I stopped. She gestured for me to keep going. Left without her suggestions, I found it more difficult to think of my own answers.

"I don't know," I said. "Um, I guess… people think I've got no feelings."

Polly was staring at me. "What do you mean by that?"

"Well, you know. I'm left-brained. I'm logical. Level-headed… so people tend to think that I'm sort of, like, an emotionless void. Kinda like a robot. Just, you know, silently complying with whatever people ask me to do."

"True?"

I thought. This time there was not a clear answer that supplied itself in my head.

"I don't know," I admitted. "I don't really know. Sometimes I think that's true. I mean, I haven't cried since…"

I trailed off. Blinked. Tried to collect my thoughts.

Don't think about that.

"I haven't cried in years," I amended. "I wake up some days and I just feel… numb inside, like there's nothing inside me at all, and I'm just empty."

72

I paused. I tried for an easygoing smile.

"But that's not the worst thing in the world, you know? I mean…" I trailed off. I was trying to find the right words to make myself sound convincing. "Not feeling anything is better than hurting."

Polly shook her head slightly. "I don't think so," she said quietly.

She didn't say anything else on the matter. She just turned around and started down the street.

"Alright," she called. "Are we gonna do this, or are you just gonna stand around all day?"

"Do I have a choice?"

"Of course you don't."

Polly was the one who rang the doorbell at every house. And she was the one who exclaimed, "Trick or treat!" at every house.

One lady was absolutely smitten by the two of us. "Oh, a little bumble bee!" she gushed. "How cute!"

Polly did a little spin for the woman to swoon over how adorable her wings were. Then the lady turned to me. She grinned; there was a gap between her two front teeth. "And what are you?"

I smiled at her blankly. "A boring dude with no costume."

She got a hoot out of that, which made me almost embarrassed I'd even made such a bad joke in the first place. Because we didn't have baskets, we walked away from each house with handfuls of candy that we shoved into our pockets and ate on our way to the next house.

Not every reaction was nearly as lively as the gap-toothed lady's. Sometimes there was nobody home, and a bowl of candy was left out on the porch with a sign that said "Take one". When I scooped up a handful, Polly slapped my hand, making me drop them back into the bowl.

"Take *one*," she chided me.

74

Most of the houses didn't open the door at all.

"They're probably looking through the peephole," I said to Polly. "And they're seeing that we're high schoolers and ignoring us on purpose. People hate it when high schoolers go trick-or-treating, you know."

This suspicion was confirmed by a man who opened the door and peered down at us with narrowed eyes from inside the house.

Polly went, "Trick or treat!"

The man went, "What?"

"Trick or treat!" Polly repeated with just as much enthusiasm.

He raised an eyebrow. "Aren't you two a little too old for that?"

"No," Polly said. "Trick-or-treating is eternal. You only get too old for it once you decide you're too old for it." She held her palm out in front of him.

The man's eyes shifted over to me. He held my gaze, and gave me a sort of skeptical smile. Expecting me to apologize on Polly's behalf and whisk her away, because I was dressed like a normal, sane high schooler, and surely I knew how ridiculous this was.

I did, in fact, know how ridiculous it was.

And I held my palm out right next to hers.

His smirk fell, souring instantly. "The *little* kids already took all the candy," he said gruffly. "Sorry."

Both of us were grinning from ear to ear as we walked away from his closed door empty-handed.

"I mean, he kind of had a point," I told Polly as we walked down the street together. "I haven't been trick-or-treating since I was in, like, third grade."

"Which is why you're boring." She poked my arm. "I go every year. It's good for the soul."

"Well, you're going to have to stop eventually. You can't be in college and still be trick-or-treating." I stopped, chuckling to myself at the image of a full-grown, adult Polly standing in a doorway wearing a bumble bee costume and a brilliant grin. *Trick-or-treat!*

Polly wasn't laughing. She was just looking at me. She raised her brow. "Now who on earth told you that?"

My laughter died on the spot. "You're kidding, right?" She wasn't— I could instantly tell by her expression, which always said everything. "Polly, don't tell me you're going to go trick-or-treating as a full-blown adult."

"I'll do it if I want to," she said, almost defiant. "It's not fair that there's a certain age where suddenly doing the things you've done your whole life are considered taboo. If you don't want to trick-or-treat anymore, then don't. But you shouldn't stop just because the world calls you childish."

"Yeah, but there's probably a reason why the world calls you childish, and maybe you should listen to those reasons."

"Who cares what everyone else thinks? If you know what you think, that's the only thing that matters. *That's* the truth." Then she stopped. She tilted her head at me. "Drew Hartford, do you know what you see in yourself?"

My mouth suddenly felt dry. I ran my tongue nervously over cracked lips.

When I finally got the courage to speak, it was her who spoke first.

"I had the feeling you didn't," she marveled. Her eyes locked with my own and neither of us looked away for a long moment.

Then she held out a chocolate bar and wagged it in front of my face. "I'll trade you for your jawbreaker."

I ended up giving her all of my candy. She took off her wings and folded them up, then wrapped the candy inside.

"I could live off this for months if I wanted to," she cheered happily. "Just eating nothing but candy for sustenance."

"You probably shouldn't do that."

"Yeah, probably." She looked up at me. "Are you sure you don't want to bring any of this home with you?"

"Absolutely."

"Not even for your parents?"

"My dad doesn't really like candy," I told her. "Or sweet things in general, really. They make his teeth ache."

"What about your mom?"

I went still. Alarms were sounding in my head. Rule one. *Don't think about it.*

"Um," I said slowly. I was trying to keep my voice as steady as possible.

Don't think.

"My mom's dead."

She stared deep into my eyes and didn't look away.

"That sucks," she told me.

And those words just rang through my head and stuck there for a while.

"I'm going to take all of this, then," Polly told me.

"Fine by me."

"This was fun."

I found myself smiling somehow. "Yeah."

"Happy Halloween."

"You know, this really has been a very happy Halloween," I remarked.

Polly's eyes shone in the dark, lit up by the dim street lamps. "Very very?"

"Very very."

She laughed. I was growing to love that sound. "Goodnight, Drew."

I watched her walk away in her yellow and black skirt, her fuzzy antennae reaching up and kissing the sky. And then suddenly I remembered something.

"Polly," I called. She stopped, turned around, looked at me. "I thought you said we were going to get through the entire neighborhood."

Polly held my gaze for a moment. She had a strangle gleam in her eye. The corners of her lips quirked up, and she turned around and started walking again.

I blinked, watching her shadowy silhouette disappear into the street. And I saw her lift her hand in the dark, her back still turned to me, and she gestured at the house next to her as she passed it.

I glanced up at it. It was only then that I realized we were standing back at the first house we'd started at. She was right. We had gotten through the entire neighborhood after all.

8

She bumped shoulders with me in the cafeteria line.

I turned around and she was standing there, staring at me with her black eyes.

"Happy Monday," Polly said.

"Happy Monday," I said back.

"You're wearing yellow today."

I glanced down at my shirt. Then back at her. "Yes, it would appear that way.

"You've never worn yellow before."

"Not in front of you."

"Why don't you wear it more often?" Polly demanded. She sounded almost annoyed. "It looks way better on you than any of your other clothes do."

I snickered a little. "Gee, thanks."

She reached across me and grabbed two pudding cups. Then placed one on my tray. Then stood up on her tiptoes and patted me on the head once. I pulled a face, even though I didn't actually mind her touch at all.

"See you in English," she said happily before walking off to her corner of the lunchroom.

I walked off to mine with my head spinning, a stupid grin on my face. *Yellow looked good on me.* I sat down at my lunch table, still smiling, and I didn't stop until Brent got up as soon as I arrived and swung his backpack over his shoulder, stalking away.

I blinked. I stared after him for a couple seconds. Then I glanced at Wallace, who instantly shrank back, becoming suddenly interested in his empty lunch tray.

"Where's he going?" I asked.

Wallace pursed his lips, still not looking at me. "Dunno," he said.

I frowned. I didn't like the way he said that. "Is he okay?"

"He's fine, he's just, um…" Wallace began wringing his hands together under the table. "Um, well, he's kind of… mad at you right now."

Of all the things I'd been expecting Wallace to say, it definitely was not *that*. My jaw dropped. *"Huh?"*

"Well, the thing is," said Wallace, "the party yesterday... you kinda disappeared on us."

"I was—" I stopped. "I left early."

"Where?"

"I just took a walk around the neighborhood."

"With Polly?"

I said nothing.

Wallace sighed. He didn't seem annoyed at all, just a bit exasperated; I knew that he and Brent had already figured that part out, and now I was just confirming it.

"He noticed both of you were gone," he explained. "He didn't talk to Jess the rest of the night, so his whole *ask-her-out-on-Halloween* plan didn't really work."

"So basically it's my fault that he chickened out."

Wallace raised his hands defensively. "I didn't say that. I'm pretty sure he's just upset and he's taking it out on you, man. But don't be surprised if he gives you the cold shoulder for the next few days."

"More like the next few weeks, knowing him," I muttered. Wallace just grimaced sympathetically.

I got up from the table and threw away my untouched lunch tray. My ears were ringing. Whatever. What did I care about Brent, anyway? It wasn't my fault he didn't have the guts to talk to Jess himself. It wasn't my fault.

It *wasn't* my fault.

And yet I couldn't stop thinking about it the whole day. Knowing that he was angry with me, it was impossible to think about anything else.

I was so unnerved by the whole thing that I hardly even glanced in Polly's direction during English. She leaned over to me at one point and whispered, "This is very boring."

I was too distracted to notice the cue. I just smiled at her half-heartedly.

She didn't return it. Instead she reached over and jabbed me in the shoulder. "You're supposed to say, 'very very'."

I still didn't bother to make eye contact with her. "My bad."

Polly sat back in her chair. She eyed me for a few seconds. "What's up with you?"

"Nothing."

"That was a lie."

Something inside me snapped. "Yes, Polly, sometimes people lie," I ground out, turning around in my seat to face her. "Sometimes people don't constantly say whatever they want to completely unfiltered because *maybe* not everyone wants the entire world to know every single thought in their head."

The words tasted sour in my mouth; I regretted them as soon as they left. I forced my eyes away from her, half-horrified at the way I'd lashed out. I *never* lashed out like that. I had no idea why I had to choose her as my first victim, of all people. And then I realized I knew exactly why, and it was the same reason that she was different than everyone else.

I kept my eyes fixed on the board, where Mrs. Pruitt stood writing down the names of literary devices we'd encounter when we began reading *Macbeth* the next day. I waited anxiously for Polly to retort, but she didn't. She had become a black hole of radio silence in the seat next to me, and while I tried to focus on what Mrs. Pruitt was saying, all I could hear was the white noise coming from Polly's seat. Every muscle in my body had gone tense. When she was talking, she was terrifying; when she was silent, she was unbearable. I was just about ready to spontaneously implode.

Until finally, she spoke:

"That was pretty jerkish of you."

Her voice didn't waver; her tone didn't change at all. I stole a glance at her and I saw that her eyes were completely dry.

The bell rang. Polly pulled her bag over her shoulder and left without saying another word to me.

I trudged along out of the classroom, my eyes fixed on my feet the entire time. Everything inside of me sagged, feeling heavier than usual. The weight made me drag my feet, and each step felt like an incredible burden.

While I was walking home, I felt something wet fall down my cheek. I frowned and wiped at it. It couldn't have been a tear, obviously. I didn't *cry.*

I felt two more drops hit my face.

And then too many to count as it began to rain, and then pour.

I sucked in my breath and picked up my pace. It was biting cold and I was wearing only a thin coat. None of it would've been nearly as bad if I wasn't getting completely soaked by the second. My umbrella was far away somewhere in my house, which was still a good couple miles away.

I could hear my sneakers squelching with every step I took. My shoes had become swamps, my socks already drowned in them. The cold made my toes numb and sent harsh shivers wracking my entire body.

My initial plan was to get home as quickly as my legs could possibly take me.

Instead, I found myself coming to a steady stop when I reached Brent's neighborhood. The street was dead silent, except for the harsh patter of rain pelting against the road.

I sighed before walking through his neighborhood gates.

Nobody answered the door when I knocked. I tried again to no avail and eventually resorted to ringing the doorbell. This time, the door swung open and his mom was standing there, her eyes lighting up when she saw me.

"Drew!" she exclaimed. "Oh, what a surprise! Hold on—"

She withdrew into the house again. "Honey!" she called. "Come here, Drew's at the door!"

I instantly felt uncomfortable. I hadn't quite prepared for a confrontation with both of them, especially not dripping wet like this. Mr. Haslett emerged from the hallway and made his way over to his wife's side.

"Drew," he greeted, a friendly twinkle in his eye. "We haven't seen you in a while. How are you?"

I tried not to let them see my teeth chattering. "Good," I said breezily. "How are you?"

"You're drenched, son," he chuckled. Kind of funny how just that single word— *son* — made my stomach feel like it'd been flipped inside out. I always felt like that around Brent's parents, though. They acted… like parents, I guess. "Come in, you must be freezing."

"You don't mind…?"

"Of course not!" the two of them gushed quickly. They immediately took me by the shoulders and wheeled me inside the house.

"Sorry," I said sheepishly, "I'm getting water everywhere. I left my umbrella at home."

"Oh, it's just water," Mrs. Haslett told me, chuckling. "What brings you here?"

"Um, I wanted to talk to Brent." I shifted my feet. "Is he here?"

"Yes, go ahead, he's in his room," Mr. Haslett said.

Brent's bedroom door was closed. I knocked twice before entering.

Brent was sitting on his bed, his head turned so that he was facing the opposite wall, away from me. He didn't budge when I walked in, didn't cast a single look in my direction.

"Hey," I said awkwardly.

He didn't say anything.

I pressed my lips together. "Come on," I practically begged. "Listen, I know you're mad, but you can't ignore me forever, dude."

"I can if I want to," Brent said petulantly. Then he turned around to face me.

Then his eyes went huge.

"What the— you're soaked!"

"Yes, I am. Because I walked all the way to your house in the rain just to apologize to you. Isn't that romantic?"

"You did?"

I nodded tiredly. "So, are we cool now?"

He pondered for a moment. "You still haven't apologized," he pointed out.

I sighed.

"Brent Haslett," I said slowly, "from the bottom of my heart, I'm sorry. I know that yesterday meant a lot to you and I should've been there for it."

Brent stared at me for a moment. Then he smiled.

"Okay," he said. "You're forgiven. We're cool."

"Cool. See you at school tomorrow."

"See you."

That was the end of our interaction. I couldn't help but feel a bit annoyed that I'd gone so far out of my way just to say sorry to him, and all because of his stupid pride. But I told myself it was the right thing to do. I knew that if I didn't apologize to him, it would just be a battle of willpower. And that was a battle that Brent could win, every single time. I had no doubt in my mind that he could hold a grudge against me until the day he was put into his grave if I let him.

At least he'd accepted my apology, though. That was all that mattered in that moment.

Brent's parents saw me out when I left.

"You can stay for dinner if you want," Mrs. Haslett offered. They followed me to the doorway.

"I'm okay. Thank you, though."

"You know you're welcome here anytime you want," Mr. Haslett told me.

Mrs. Haslett nodded eagerly in agreement. "You should come over for dinner sometime," she said. "And bring your dad with you. We'd love to see him."

"Okay."

"Are you two… you know. Doing alright?" Mr. Haslett asked.

I hated that question with every fiber of my being. Even though I wanted to scream, I just nodded politely. "Yeah, we're fine."

He smiled. "Well, if you ever need someone to talk to…"

I hated *that* even more.

It was just about the most empty, meaningless thing you could say to a person. In the three years that Mom had been gone, I'd grown to hate the sympathy offered by others. People were always telling me that everything was going to get better, that they understood what I was going through, that they were here for me. How did they know any of those things?

People could say they understood, but they didn't. They just didn't. They could offer their help, but it meant absolutely nothing if they weren't actually going to be there through the tough moments.

But I knew Brent's parents meant well. So I just smiled and told them "thank you".

"Have a nice evening," I said to them.

"Oh, you're too sweet," Mrs. Haslett cooed. "What a nice boy you are, Drew."

Yup, that seemed to be the general consensus.

We waved our goodbyes before I went back out. The rain had died down to a soft drizzle, though I was still dripping wet and my shoes were squeaking all the same.

I sneezed once on the way home. After that first one, I fell subject to an uncontrollable frenzy of sneezing. My head began to feel sort of light, like a balloon, making me dizzy.

I dismissed it. I was just cold, that was all. I was sure I'd be feeling back to normal by morning.

So my initial plan was to go straight home as fast as my legs could possibly take me. But once more, I found myself straying from the plan.

As I walked home, I passed by the thrift store. In the front of the store on display was a mannequin wearing a yellow button-up polo shirt.

I stopped in my tracks. I stared at it for a few moments, rain dripping down onto my face.

I found myself walking inside. The store was empty except for me. I guess most normal people didn't walk to the thrift store in the pouring rain.

I scrounged every aisle, every rack, sifting through all the clothes manically. I was like a dog, sniffing out all of the items, my nose tuned to one color only.

I gathered up every single yellow thing I could find in my arms and unloaded it over the counter.

What a mess I must've looked to the cashier, a scraggly, rain-soaked boy peeking out over a mound of sunny yellow fabric, dumping out the contents of his wallet and blurting out "I'll take all of these, please, you can keep the change".

9

As it turned out, I wasn't feeling back to normal by morning.

I woke drenched in sweat, lying in my bed in damp sheets. Despite the fact that I seemed to be on fire, I was freezing cold, shivering painfully.

I managed to stumble out of my bed. As I got ready for school, the world swam in and out of focus. A million different diamond specks shimmered before my eyes. My head felt way too heavy, throbbing atop my shoulders, and my legs trembled a little when I walked.

I made my way downstairs. I was so disoriented that it was really a wonder I didn't lose my balance and tumble down the staircase. I shoved all of my things into my backpack, my ears ringing.

...ew? Drew?

"Drew?"

I blinked slowly. I glanced up and saw that my dad was watching me from the dining table, over the rim of his coffee mug.

"Yeah?" I said. My voice cracked a bit. I sounded unmistakably like a frog.

"I called your name a few times," Dad said slowly. "Hey, you look kinda..." He gestured at his face. "Pale. Are you alright?"

"Yeah, yeah, I'm fine."

"Your voice is..."

"I'm okay," I insisted. "I'll see you after school, Dad."

Once more, I closed the door on him while he was still saying goodbye to me.

I sneezed the entire walk to school. Every fiber of my being ached and died with each passing second. Part of me wanted to just drive myself to school and save myself the exhaustion of walking, but anything was better than driving, I reminded myself. Anything was better than driving because *don't think about it.*

So I dragged my feet all throughout the day, lumbering along to each of my classes. Luckily, Brent was back at the lunch table and as talkative as ever, so I didn't need to use too much energy when it came to socializing.

But then English rolled around and I remembered all at once what had happened with Polly yesterday. More accurately, what had happened with *me*. I sat down in my seat next to her and she didn't look in my direction. That alone was almost certainly an indication of just how much she probably hated my guts now.

I'd undoubtedly be hearing all sorts of nasty things about myself soon, knowing her knack for spreading hidden truths about people. I could practically hear her voice in the hallway, whispering in everyone's ears. *Hey, you know Drew Hartford, the "nice" boy? Boy, do I have news for you.*

Deep down I knew that was just me talking, though. Anything that happened in your head was a conversation between you and yourself. But I couldn't help but worry, sitting there next to Polly and her awful radio silence the entire class period.

That is, until Mrs. Pruitt jarred me back to reality by saying, "I want you all to turn to your table partner and read the first scene out loud with each other."

I deflated instantly, sagging lower into my seat. As we took out our copies of *Macbeth*, I knew that this encounter could only be disastrous. Dread began seeping in at the corners of my heart as I turned slowly to Polly.

And she said, "Alright, I'm doing the first page."

And she just jumped right into it without giving me a second to react.

"*'When shall we three meet again?'*" she said. She was reading as the witches, so she was putting on this horrible, hyena-like voice to match the character. It was so abrupt and shocking that I couldn't stop an involuntary grin from breaking out across my face. Underneath the witch voice, though, I realized she'd also taken up a strange sort of dialect to the verse. *"'In thunder, lightning, or in rain?'"*

"What—" I was laughing uncontrollably now. "Are you doing an accent?"

"It's British," she informed me. "The play takes place in England, Drew. Read a book for once."

"*Macbeth* takes place in Scotland."

She stopped and was silent for a moment.

"Well," she said finally, "that can be arranged."

She started again, this time with a thick, poor Scottish accent: *"'When the hurly burly's done, when the battle's lost and won…'"*

I watched her, fascinated, while she read. It was like yesterday had never even happened. Everything was going absolutely fine— better than fine, really, because I still couldn't believe how amazing Polly was after weeks of being around her— but then her voice started to become more and more distant, until it sounded like I was underwater and she was somewhere above the surface.

I blinked a couple times, but it felt sluggish. The entire world seemed like it had slowed down. I tried to focus on Polly's voice again, but she kept slipping away.

And then my stomach lurched.

I stood up so quickly that I almost knocked my chair over in my haste. Polly looked alarmed, jumping back and staring up at me in confusion. She stopped reading. "Sorry," I mumbled before turning and walking as quickly as I could to the front of the room.

I heard my voice ask Mrs. Pruitt if I could go to the bathroom. She said yes and then I felt my legs pedaling me out of the classroom, although they were shaking like mad and could hardly hold my weight up.

Everything drifted away for a while. I saw the blur of classrooms as I rushed down the hall. The entire world was spinning rapidly. I walked into a wall and slammed my head against a locker and said *sorry* to it. All this while feeling almost like I was dreaming, like none of this was real. My head was still throbbing. My ears had begun to ring again.

When my vision finally came back into focus and my head had stopped reeling, I was bent over a toilet bowl, throwing up everything in my stomach. It was mostly just acid, burning my throat as it came up, making me wince.

Once I finished it took all of the strength in my body not to slump to the ground. My hands were shaking as I flushed the toilet, but even then I still sat on the tile floor, breathing heavy and feeling absolutely drained.

Nothing else came up after a few minutes. The throbbing in my head died down, so I stood up and wobbled over to the sink.

I washed my hands. I scrubbed water over my face, then rinsed my mouth out until the bad taste was gone.

Then I looked up, locking eyes with my reflection in the mirror.

He stared back at me, a gaunt-looking skeleton, complete with deep circles under his eyes. It was only then, with me staring at him and him staring at me, that I realized just how much I hated him, that ugly, horrible creature that I saw every time I looked in the mirror.

I heard Polly's voice, close, like she was talking into my ear. I imagined her standing before me in her bumble bee skirt on Halloween night, the street empty save for the two of us. *Do you know what you see in yourself?*

I looked back at my reflection.

And I saw this awful, wretched thing, a pathetic doormat just waiting to be stepped on some more, a silent, compliant son who never spoke up for himself. Yes, I hated him. He hated me right back.

Experimentally, I forced my mouth into a toothy smile. When I was smiling, I noticed that the bags under my eyes seemed a bit softer, and my features a bit smoother. I kept the smile on for a few seconds, trying to burn it into my face's muscle memory, before finally letting it drop.

I turned away and walked out of the bathroom. Almost as soon as I stepped outside, Polly was standing there leaning against the wall of the boy's bathroom.

"Hey," she said.

"Oh my god." She snickered to herself as I stumbled back, startled. "Were you standing there the whole time?"

"Just long enough to hear you vomiting your guts out." Polly stepped out into the open, her hands clasped behind her back. "Which, by the way, gross. Are you sick or something?"

"No."

"As if I believe you." Polly tilted her head at me. "You're not gonna pass out on me or anything, right?"

"No." Again, I wasn't super confident. "Sorry I interrupted your performance of *Macbeth*."

She shook her head, making a *tsk* sound at me. "You could've just told me if you didn't like my Scottish accent."

"As much as I wish that was the case." I straightened a bit. "Well, back to class."

"About that." Polly's eyes glinted mischievously in a way that made me feel like I was floating. Or maybe that was just my head pounding. "What do you say we make a little detour before going back?"

"A *detour?*" I echoed. "You mean, like, you want to ditch?"

"It's not ditching," she argued. "I have a hall pass." Just to prove it she held up Mrs. Pruitt's class lanyard in front of my face.

I examined it as best I could with her swinging it inches from my nose. It was legit. "Mrs. Pruitt actually gave that to you?"

"I told her I had to go to the bathroom."

My jaw dropped. "You lied?"

"No. We're at the bathroom, aren't we?" Polly dropped the lanyard back down to her side. "Now let's go."

"Where are we going, again?" I wondered aloud as I followed her down the empty hallway.

"Surprise." She swung the lanyard back and forth as she walked.

Even though the voice in the back of my head kept reminding me that we were still *technically* ditching class and we could definitely get into trouble for this, I found myself following her anyway. I had no control over my legs. I just walked. And walked, until we finally arrived at our location.

"The library?" I said, skeptical.

"Don't you know what's happening here?" Polly said.

I shook my head. She looked rather pleased that I didn't know; she clicked her tongue at me condescendingly.

"Book fair," she informed me.

I barked out a laugh. "The *book fair?* Polly, nobody goes to the book fair."

"Looks like we're nobody for today, then."

She grabbed me and hauled me inside. I followed her without complaint.

"We have to be quiet," she whispered as we walked in, "don't wanna raise any suspicion—"

She stopped when the door closed behind us and we were standing together inside the empty library. Her eyes were huge, flitting back and forth almost feverishly as she took in her surroundings.

I frowned. "Polly?"

"This is a big library," she said in a hushed, awestruck voice. "Biggest book fair I've ever been to."

I glanced back around myself. Our library didn't seem like anything out of the ordinary. But then again, Polly's definition of ordinary was a bit different than everyone else's. I remembered what she'd said the first day she transferred to English. She used to live in....

"Eagle River," I said. She looked at me. "Did you ever have book fairs there?"

"Yeah." She glanced back around herself, took a few steps aimlessly around the library. "Only in elementary school, though. I didn't even know high schools did book fairs."

"Eldridge is the only high school I know that still does them," I told her. "People don't really take well to change around here."

"Yeah." Polly was still staring at the library in silent awe. "My elementary school book fair wasn't even half the size of this one."

We walked to the first couple of tables, which were set up with mostly classics. I thumbed through a few mindlessly.

"These are all boring books," she said. "Boo." She picked a couple up. "*Anne of Green Gables... The Picture of Dorian Gray...*"

Polly fake gagged. Then she broke out into laughter and looked at me.

"Those are good books," I said, only somewhat defensive. I took *The Picture of Dorian Gray* from her and eyed it carefully.

110

"Dude, this cover used to haunt me at night when I was a kid."

I felt her staring at me as I ran my fingers over the smooth paper front. "You've actually read these?" she asked incredulously.

"You haven't?"

"Of course not. They're books that everyone knows about but no one actually reads because they're so boring."

"If you've never read it, how do you know it's boring?"

Polly snatched the copy of *Dorian Gray* back from me, and held it sideways, flipping pointedly through the pages. "The *length*," she said very seriously.

We both broke into laughter, then took to shushing each other obnoxiously as we went on to the next table.

"You're very weird, you know," she informed me as we went through the next set of books. They were all young adult romance, a genre I was less familiar with, but still had my fair dabbles in. "It's not super often you meet someone who's totally into reading." She picked a book up and looked over it with zero interest.

"Reading is fun."

She glared at me over a paperback cover of *The Fault in Our Stars* she was clutching with both hands. "Take it back."

"Why don't you like reading?"

"That's what movies are for," she told me. "Movies get the same exact story across, but with a mere *fraction* of the work it takes to read a book."

I laughed. "That's not true at all."

Polly turned to me. "Really," she said. "How so?"

She lowered the book cover, looking at me full-on now. She waited expectantly for me to continue.

"Well," I said. "Um. It's just… okay, so it seems like a movie tells the same exact story as a book, but the thing is that there are different aspects to both that get lost in translation when you switch to the other. Like, it's incredibly hard to reach the same level of visual imagery through words that you can by just *showing* someone a picture on a screen. In that sense, a movie would be superior, right? Except there's more to it, because there's something about the written word that's got this beautiful fragility— if you arrange words in a certain way, put them in a specific ordered pattern, that changes everything about how the reader views them. And so when a reader is able to *feel* something, feel real emotions just by reading a bunch of words on paper, that's incredible. There's nothing like it. I..."

I stopped myself. I realized she was staring at me, unblinking and unwavering. I swallowed tightly.

"Sorry," I said, sheepish. "That got pretty boring."

Polly shook her head firmly. "Of all things, Drew Hartford, you are not *boring*," she told me. "And you wanna know something? That is the first time you've actually talked to me without hiding anything. You just said everything in your head and didn't care how you sounded out loud."

I blinked. I realized distantly that she was right. She must have recognized that realization on my face, because she beamed at me and said, "How did that feel?"

"Good," I admitted.

She jabbed a finger at me. "Exactly."

We moved on from the Y/A. Polly skipped ahead, rushing to the next table.

"Now this is what I came for," she exclaimed, delighted.

The table was bustling with exotic-looking knick-knacks and trinkets. There were boxes full of erasers molded into strange little shapes, scented pencils, little wall posters—and there was some weird stuff, too, like *weird* weird. There was one box that had these sticks with little plastic hands at the end of them. Polly lunged for those immediately. She picked up one and poked me with the fake hand.

"I used to be *addicted* to these things as a kid," she told me.

"These things?" I repeated, mildly horrified. "What do you even do with these?"

"In my head I had a lot of cooler uses for them. I always dreamed of being a teacher and using this to get their attention." She gestured with the little pointer finger sticking into the air in no particular direction. "Like, 'alright kids, eyes on the board now'."

"But you have… you know. Regular hands to do that."

Polly grinned. "Now what's the fun in that?" She put the pointer finger down and grabbed one of the scented pencils. She took a sniff, then held it out for me to smell.

"Grape," she told me.

I sniffed. Then I scrunched my face up in disgust. "Ugh," I said. "That does *not* smell like grape."

"What does it smell like?"

115

"I dunno. Vomit."

"Yeah, *you* would know."

We were laughing again. Then shushing each other again. She put the pencil back and started in on the erasers.

"Hey," I realized suddenly. "Polly."

"Yeah."

"I didn't apologize for yesterday."

She paused. "Yeah," she repeated.

"I'm sorry," I told her. "I was stressed out but I took it out on you and that wasn't cool. You were right. That was a jerkish thing for me to say."

Polly picked up an eraser that was shaped like a little lollipop. She examined it with some interest. "So you didn't mean what you said?"

"No," I said quickly. "I mean... I don't know. I didn't mean that you're weird or bad or anything like that. But I do think you're... different. You're not like...."

"I'm not like other girls?" she suggested, eyeing me suspiciously.

"No," I said. "God, no. You're not like any other living creature on the planet. Don't limit yourself to just *girls.*"

Polly's eyes glittered. "And you mean that?"

"Yeah, I do. I mean, you're… you're… you know. You're amazing. And terrifying. Both at the same time somehow."

She grabbed a pair of plastic glasses with bushy eyebrows and a fake nose and mustache plastered around the frames. She slid them on over her face and looked at me.

"You're scared of me?" she teased.

"Yes," I said without missing a beat. "Polly Park, you scare me more than anything in the entire world. You scare me senseless. Sometimes I don't even know if you're real."

Polly took the glasses off. She reached over and poked me in the arm.

"I'm real," she assured me. Then she added, "See, I used my regular hand just to show it."

117

10

By the time school ended, the nausea and dizziness had returned and were back to their full effect.

I started walking home. The ground under me tilted back and forth with every step I took. I'd only crossed two streets when my breathing became labored and I found myself bent over my knees, taking in ragged breaths and shivering. Sweat broke out all across my forehead and the back of my neck.

I pulled out my phone, pressed a few digits, held it to my ear. My eyelids slid shut and white spots danced behind them.

Please pick up. Please pick up.

A short burst of static, and then:

"Hello?"

"Dad," I croaked. I sneezed once. "Do you think you can pick me up? I'm... I'm at..."

I looked up. My vision had split into threes, but I managed to make out the street sign over my head. "I'm at Simon Street and I'm feeling kinda sick."

Dad was silent for a moment. "Drew, listen," he said, and I already knew it was a lost cause. I closed my eyes. "I'm waiting on a really important phone call right now, and if I leave…"

"No, I get it," I said. "Uh, sorry."

"I can get you," he said, but the offer didn't sound very open at all. He chuckled a little. "I mean, are you dying?"

Maybe. "No. I'm fine." I fought back the urge to sneeze again. "I can walk. Sorry for bothering you."

"Drew—"

I hung up before he could say anything else. I peeled my eyes open. Everything seemed too bright.

I started walking again. I must have looked like a zombie, tripping over my own feet as I made my way clumsily down the sidewalk.

The sky was swelling bigger and bigger like a balloon as I walked towards it. At one point I became certain it would swallow me whole. My teeth began to chatter once more. My bones turned to jelly in my legs.

It usually took me thirty minutes to walk home from school. I'd been wobbling around aimlessly for a solid forty-five when I heard my dad calling my name.

Disoriented, I blinked a few times in his direction, waiting for my vision to fade into focus. He was sitting in the car, pulled up next to the sidewalk beside me. His window was rolled down.

"Drew," he said. His face looked concerned for some reason.

I waved at him.

"Did you not hear me honking?" he asked.

"You were honking?" I heard myself say.

"I've been off the phone for a while," Dad told me. "I was starting to get worried that you still hadn't come home."

"I'm fine, I'm fine." I gestured passively. "No need to worry about me."

My legs were still walking. Dad got out of the car now. Somehow he caught up to me easily and grabbed me by the shoulder, stopping me.

"Hey," he said in a soft, soothing voice. I liked that a lot. He always used to use that voice on me when I was little. "Let's go home, okay? I'm gonna take you home." He placed the back of his palm on my forehead. It was freezing cold to the touch; I hissed and pulled away. "Jesus, you're burning up."

"I can walk," I insisted. "I'm fine. I'm fine. I'm fine."

Black was starting to eat away at the corners of my vision.

"Come on," Dad said. He took me by the shoulders, turned me towards the car. "Get in."

"I'm fine, I'm fine, I'm fine," I babbled, trying to wave him off. "I'm *okayyy*."

And then the entire world went dark and I drifted away.

11

I woke up to flames licking the edge of my bed.

I tried to scream, but it came out a strangled, pathetic cry. I scrambled back, but there was nowhere to go. The fire had eaten up my entire mattress— it was sweltering and nipping away at my skin. I was melting, blisters and burns bubbling all across my bare arms, my face, my neck. The heat was unbearable, the smoke suffocating.

A face came into focus above mine. A knit brow, tightly pressed lips. I knew that face.

"Dad," I gasped out.

"Hey," he said. "Calm down, alright? Everything's fine. You're okay."

"Fire," I sputtered. "There's— there's fire—"

I was dimly aware of a frantic, high-pitched beeping noise somewhere in the distance.

"You're okay," he repeated. "You're okay."

I realized with a panic that he sounded strangely familiar. And that was because he sounded like *me*.

"*No,*" I cried. "No, I'm not okay! I'm not okay, Dad! Don't you see that everything's burning?"

And Dad—

Dad shushed me.

I was burning and dying and falling and he *shushed* me. I had never been more horrified.

"You're just hallucinating," he said in a calm voice. "It's the fever."

"No," I heard myself say. "No, no, no, no, no." It turned into wailing, and then I felt wetness on my cheeks. My vision blurred. I looked up. It must've been this stupid rain.

Except it wasn't, because instead of a stormy sky, I found myself staring up at a blank white ceiling. And I knew that I was crying, and those were tears spilling down my face, not raindrops.

Weird. I didn't cry. At least, I hadn't cried since…

12

When I woke up my dad was shaking me by the shoulders.

"Drew," he was saying. "Drew. Wake up."

I blinked groggily and glanced at my clock. 3:49 AM. I frowned, confused. "What's goin' on?" I slurred.

My vision came into focus. I saw that my dad was crying.

"Your mom," he started.

He never finished.

We drove to the emergency room together. He was crying the entire way there. I was too terrified to make sense of anything. Everything inside of me went numb.

Dad never told me what happened. I only figured the truth out through fragments of things I picked up from the doctors.

There'd been a car accident. It wasn't anybody's fault. There was nobody to blame. Mom was driving home from the airport late at night. She was going down an icy road and lost control of the wheels. The car spiraled. Hit a tree.

And of course, there was my mom herself. Lying very still on a hospital bed, face beaten and bruised, eyes closed and swollen shut, wires and tubes sticking out of her, lips parted but not breathing— why wasn't she breathing? They strapped an oxygen mask over her blackened, beaten face. It made her even more unrecognizable than she already was.

I tried to convince myself that it wasn't really my mom lying there. It couldn't be. No, my mom was beautiful, her skin like porcelain, perfect and unmarked. Mom was radiant. She was always smiling. Mom loved the stars; Mom *was* a star. She was not this broken, mangled thing lying unmoving on her back, an oxygen mask concealing her warm smile, a tube forced down her throat to coax air into her useless lungs.

But even then she couldn't breathe. I listened to the awful, high-pitched beeping of her heart monitor while doctors swarmed past me, all elbowing their way to her bedside.

My dad turned away. He couldn't look.

Me, on the other hand, all I could do *was* look.

"I'm going to ask you to leave now," a nurse requested.

Dad took me by the shoulders with trembling hands and led me out of the hospital room. As the door closed, I heard the beeping go very still.

And then there was no more beeping, just a single note that screeched awfully into the silence behind that closed door, and I listened to my mother's heart stop.

13

I woke up a third time to complete silence.

I warily checked my blankets, my legs, searching the mattress for any signs of fire. I found that I wasn't hot anymore, though. My covers were drenched in sweat, but I felt more cold than anything.

Mom wasn't in the hospital bed, either, I realized. I was the one in the hospital bed. I was alone. And my heart monitor was still beeping steadily beside me, which I became aware of with a sinking feeling of what I couldn't distinguish between relief and disappointment.

The door opened and a nurse entered the room. Her curly hair was pulled back into a loose bun. It was nice, I thought somewhere in the dull space of my brain.

"Good evening," she said with a smile. Her voice was so soft I hardly heard it. "Your fever's broken. That's a good sign."

"How long have I been here?" I asked her.

"You've been drifting in and out of consciousness for almost two days now," she told me.

I glanced to the side of the room, where there was a big glass window covered by a thin curtain. It was nighttime. There were no stars out.

"You were delirious. Do you remember anything that happened when you were awake?"

I was crying. I cautiously touched my cheek with my hand. Dry. Thank god.

"No, I don't remember anything," I lied.

"That's pretty common, so there's no need to worry about that."

"What's wrong with me?"

"Just a bad ear infection. They often develop from common colds."

"An *ear infection?*" I repeated in disbelief. *That* was what had put me down for the count? It sounded way too stupid and harmless to have wreaked that much havoc on my immune system. I had been a

128

complete wreck, practically comatose for two days, burning from fever and vomiting and crying and hallucinating. I felt like I'd just died and come back. How could that all have been a tiny ear infection?

The nurse seemed to read the skepticism on my face. "If you stayed home and rested when you first began feeling symptoms," she chided me, "you would've had a much smoother recovery. You did quite a number on yourself, going to school and walking around like that."

She placed her stethoscope over my chest. It was cold.

"Breathe in," she told me. I breathed in. "Out." I breathed out.

"Is my dad here?" I asked.

"Outside. I'll go get him for you."

She left the room and the door shut with a click. When she returned, my dad followed her inside.

"His vitals are stable," she was saying to him. "He's free to go home whenever you want."

"Great," Dad said. He sounded exhausted. "Alright, Drew. Let's get going, yeah?"

I nodded, but I couldn't meet his gaze.

I waited in a stiff plastic chair in the lobby while Dad signed me out. I felt numb everywhere; I was only distantly aware of the cold. I wrapped my arms subconsciously around myself.

Once Dad was finished, he walked back over to me. I stood up. We both just stood before each other for a moment.

I waited for him to embrace me, to start crying and tell me how scared he was, how glad he was that I was okay.

Instead, he just sort of made this deep sighing sound and nodded at me.

"Let's go," he said. His eyes were tired.

We didn't say anything when we walked out of the hospital and into the silence of the night air. We didn't say anything when we walked through the parking lot and to the car.

Dad got into the driver's seat. I got into the passenger's. I closed my door, fastened my seatbelt.

Dad put the keys into the ignition. I listened to the car whirring to life beneath me, humming quietly and running in place.

Then Dad said, "Drew, I would have picked you up if you told me how bad it was."

I pursed my lips, staying silent. Dad didn't look at me. His gaze was fixed somewhere far beyond his window.

"You know that, right?" he said. "You know I would've come to get you."

But you haven't.

"Yeah," I said quietly. My eyes fluttered shut. "Yeah, I know."

The accident wasn't anybody's fault.

I knew it wasn't.

That didn't stop me from imagining all the different ways it could have gone.

It always kept me up at night. My mom's flight home had gotten delayed; that was the reason she was driving so late to begin with. If that airline had just sent out their airplane on time, maybe she'd be able to see the ice along the road and she'd slow down first. Maybe if her boss hadn't called her out of town to work, then she wouldn't have even left home.

The worst one of all, though, was maybe— maybe if my dad had been the one driving that night instead of my mom— maybe if he'd been the dead one, my mom would still be able to love me after.

I hated whenever that idea showed up lurking in the shadowy corners of my mind, hated it more than any of the other screwed up thoughts in my head. Because I knew that if Mom was still here, maybe I'd really be okay, instead of just having to pretend all the time.

I knew Dad loved me. It just wasn't the same. Dad was terrified. He didn't touch me,

didn't talk to me, didn't look at me.
Completely lost in his own head.

Don't you see that everything's burning?

Don't you see that I'm falling, Dad?

Maybe he couldn't. Maybe he couldn't
because I was the one pretending the fire was
never there to begin with.

14

Polly was the first person I saw when I made my spectacular comeback at school.

"Jesus," she said, walking up to me, "I thought you were dead."

"Surprise."

"What happened to you? Took sick days?"

"Yup."

"Well, I hope you know that we got through the entire first act of *Macbeth* reading out loud."

"You had to read out loud to yourself?"

"No. I had to partner with Connor Brightfield. He hated my voices."

"So I'm a step up."

"I mean, he didn't dip on me to throw up in the bathroom, so." Polly shrugged. "It's a toss-up."

I lazily mimicked being shot through the heart. "I'm hurt."

"I'm glad you're back." Her eyes lit up. "I'm very glad."

"Very very?"

"Very *very.*" The morning bell rang; Polly looped her arm through mine. "What's your first class?"

"Spanish."

"I have history. That's on the way." She tugged on my arm. "Walk with me."

I obeyed without hesitation.

"You should've heard all my voices," she told me. "You only got to hear the witches—they're cool, but boy, my Lady Macbeth is a real showstopper. My Banquo's pretty good too…"

As we walked through the hallway, I began to notice that people were staring. For a few selfish seconds I thought it was because we must have looked like a couple, with her arm laced through mine, and high schoolers loved to stare at couples in the halls.

But then I remembered just *who* was hanging on my arm. And I knew instantly that this wasn't about me at all. They were all looking at her.

135

Hallways were always an ordeal, packed in tight and overflowing with hurried students, all elbowing past one another to get to class. When we walked that morning, the crowd parted like the Red Sea. It was as if Polly had some disease that everyone was terrified of catching, and I was just the idiot who kept getting in her face and was surely going to get infected too, now.

"Why is everyone looking at you like that?" I asked her in a hushed voice.

Polly blinked innocently at me. "Could be a lot of different things," she said in a roundabout way. "You can never really be sure which one."

I opened my mouth to question her again, but she slipped her arm out from mine and stepped to the side.

"This is where I get off," she said. She saluted me. "See you in English, deputy."

Apparently, I *had* been infected. People kept their distance from me during class. I asked a kid if I could borrow a pen and he

136

looked scared out of his mind by the mere fact that I'd spoken to him. When I was done using his pen I tried to give it back to him and he refused it, insisting I kept it.

Of course. I'd contaminated his pen, now. I felt like an alien in my own skin walking around school, knowing everyone else knew that Polly and I were friends.

Friends, and… of course, there was that other thing.

She liked me.

"What's wrong with everyone?" I demanded when I sat down with Brent and Wallace.

"So you're not dead," Brent marveled.

"We all thought you were dead," Wallace said.

"What's wrong with everyone?" I repeated readily.

Wallace frowned. "What do you mean?"

"I mean, why is everyone staring at Polly like she's got a third eye?"

Brent rolled his eyes. "You're just noticing now that she's weird?"

"Of course I know she's weird. Everyone knows that. But they never avoided her like she had the plague before."

"Lola and Jake broke up," Wallace said.

I blinked. That was a sentence I hadn't been expecting. "Uh. Okay?"

Brent stared at me. "Because of Polly."

I furrowed my brow. *"What?"* I enunciated.

"She saw Jake kissing Phoebe behind the gym lockers," Wallace explained, "and she told everyone. Including Lola. So now everyone's in a state of total chaos…"

"All thanks to her," Brent finished. "It's *bad*, Drew. Everyone's been giving Phoebe crap for it, Jake's pissed, Lola's in a state of depression— all because *Polly* couldn't keep herself from running her mouth."

It was too horrible to be true. "She wouldn't do that," I protested. "She's… you know, she's honest—"

138

"*Brutally* honest," Brent put in.

I frowned. "Fine," I said. "But she's not heartless. She's a real person with real feelings. She wouldn't *do* that."

"How do you know?"

"I— because she— she—"

I stopped. I was unable to form words properly— they were whirling around incomprehensibly in my blender of a brain, spinning in a hazy blur.

They were right. There really was no way for me to know what Polly would or wouldn't do. I could spend as much time with her as I wanted but I would never understand what went on in her mind.

Was there a boundary that existed anywhere in her head? Were there any lines she wouldn't cross? What was that invisible force in her throat that allowed all of the forbidden words and phrases in the world to leave her tongue?

During English, Polly was practically bouncing up and down with excitement when she saw me. She already had *Macbeth* sitting open on her lap. "Okay, okay," she said. "Listen to this, ready? Here's Banquo—"

"Polly," I said.

She stopped. She looked at me, her smile dropping instantly. She must have sensed the seriousness in my tone. "Yes?"

"Did you tell everyone that Jake was cheating on Lola?"

Polly thought for a second. Then she said confidently, "No."

I couldn't believe it. For all her talk of honesty, she was really going to deny this to my face? "That's a *lie*," I said, unable to keep the venom from seeping into my voice.

Now her eyes went huge, her brow furrowing. *"No!"* she exclaimed, so loudly that the other kids sitting near us turned and looked at us. "You think I would lie to you about something stupid like that?"

"Nobody would even *look* in our direction when we walked to class today," I told her. "Wallace and Brent told me what happened."

"I didn't *lie*," Polly protested. I'd never seen her unraveled like this, eyes wide and almost frantic, like a deer caught in headlights. "I didn't tell *everyone* what I saw. I told Jess, because she *asked* me, and then she was the one who told everyone and said that I told *her*."

"I—" My mouth shut with a snap. I considered what she said, and found I had nothing left to retort. "Oh."

"Yeah. *Oh*." Polly glared at me. "You're really dumb for a smart person, you know."

"So then it's Jess's fault," I said. "That's not fair. She was the one who spread the news but you're the one being blamed."

"Don't be childish," Polly clucked. "The blame-game is for people who can't accept the fact that some things aren't the fault of one bad person."

"Because it's easier to blame somebody."

141

She nodded. "But that doesn't make it right."

"Still…" I sucked in a breath between clenched teeth. "You're going to keep being friends with Jess after she did this to you?"

"What did she do, exactly?" She said it like a challenge.

"Threw you under the bus."

"No, she told the truth," Polly said. "I was the one who told her what happened."

I couldn't believe her. All this time I'd spent with her and I still couldn't *believe* her. "Are you serious?" I asked. "Polly, don't you think some truths shouldn't be told?"

"No," she said. I was surprised by how confidently she said that, without any signs of hesitation.

I stared at her. *"Why?"* I said. I just couldn't understand her. "Are you trying to be morally upright or what? Do you just live your life around the whole 'honesty is the best policy' thing or something?"

She shrugged. "Your definition of morally upright is not the same as mine," she said simply.

"Yeah, but you still care about people's feelings, don't you? I mean, you can't always just say what you're thinking. Haven't you ever heard of white lies?"

Polly shook her head at me. "White lies don't exist," she said. "They're just *lies*, Drew."

"Yeah, but Lola and Jake..." I paused. "Their relationship is done, Polly. Like, *done.* Don't— don't you feel bad about that at all?"

Polly thought for a moment. "No," she said again, decidedly. "Because I couldn't live with myself if I knew that someone was being cheated on and I never said anything. Even if everyone else hates me for it."

I wanted to comfort her. I wanted to tell her that nobody hated her, that the world was her best friend, but we both knew that was just another lie.

"The truth hurts sometimes," I told her. "I think that's what scares people."

"It still scares you."

"Yeah."

"But do you care?"

"About what?"

"About all the things I say?"

She watched me closely, waiting for me to answer. I knew she would be able to sense the lie in anything I said, just like she always could. But I found that an answer came surprisingly easily, and I didn't even have to cover it up.

"No."

The way she smiled at me, I swear, it was like I'd just hung the stars.

15

She took me to her house after school.

My head still spins when I think about it. She took me to her house. Polly Park, the fire-breathing, nine-headed Hydra— the glowing, ten-foot-tall Unicorn— the monster, the mermaid, who was terrifying and amazing all at once, took me to her *house.*

Polly was the kind of person who showed up everywhere, but nobody ever considered exactly where she came from. In my mind I tried to imagine what kind of fantastical lair she would have resided in. I thought she might live in a cave, a shack, maybe a cupboard under some stairs or some remote haunted mansion.

It turned out I was wrong. Polly lived in a medium-sized suburban house in a small, circular neighborhood. It had a reddish-brown roof and was painted beige everywhere else, except the door, which was navy blue. She unlocked it with her own pair of keys, from which dangled a little plastic rodent keychain.

"Is that a weasel?" I'd asked her.

Polly was immediately offended. "It's a *meerkat*," she said, frowning at me. She swung the door open. "My parents got it for me at the zoo."

I followed her inside the house. "You like meerkats?"

"They're okay. My parents love them."

Polly stopped, turned around and faced me. She looked down at my feet, then back at me.

"Shoes off," she ordered.

I blinked. Glancing down, I saw that there was a shoe rack next to my foot. She'd already kicked off her sneakers and placed them onto the rack; I followed suit, feeling kind of embarrassed I hadn't done it earlier. I wasn't used to people taking their shoes off inside the house.

"Meerkats are my parents' favorite animal," Polly continued as we walked

146

inside. "They always used to want a meerkat as a pet, but they're not exactly the most ideal animals. Always digging holes. That's why bumble bees are my favorite animal."

I frowned. "Bumble—" I stopped myself.

What a bizarre thing to say. I didn't know anyone who said their favorite animal was a bumble bee. When were bees even considered animals, anyway?

I thought meerkats weren't such a huge step up, either. I'd never met anyone who said meerkats were their favorite animal. But then again, I was almost *certain* that her parents would be mildly insane. Kids were products of parenting, right? That meant Polly had to come from *somewhere.* I liked Polly, of course, but that didn't mean her behavior had become any less peculiar to me. So when I followed her into the living room and her parents were sitting on the couch together, I wasn't expecting them to look so *normal.*

They looked like her, I guessed, the same smooth skin complexion and unkempt eyebrows, pursed lips, black hair and eyes. Neither of them got up to greet us, but both of them said hello to me from the couch.

Mrs. Park asked me, "What's your name?"

"I told you, Mom, this is Drew," Polly said.

"Hi," I said. "Nice to meet you."

"Oh, Drew," said Mr. Park. He smiled at me. "So you're Polly's special friend."

I felt my face getting hot. I glanced at Polly, but she seemed unfazed by this.

She must have told him that herself, right? What did she mean by that?

I was her *special friend*. Probably because she liked me.

Oh boy. I was in deeper than ever. Here I was in her living room, meeting her parents, for god's sake.

Polly was giggling next to me. "You see that bowl between them?"

I looked. A large ceramic bowl was seated on the couch next to her parents. "Yeah?"

"It's filled with my candy," she said. "From *Halloween*. We still haven't finished it."

"Why don't you two come over here and sit with us?" Mrs. Park asked from the room.

Before I could say anything, Polly responded for me. "No thanks." I looked at her. "They're watching the softball tournament," she said, rolling her eyes. "Sports. Gross. Let's go, I want to show you something."

Polly hauled me past the living room to a sliding glass door in the back of the house. She unlocked it and slid it open before pulling me outside with her.

Her backyard was huge, but it seemed like they'd done a pretty good job filling up the space. The entire place was teeming with flowers and plant life. The scent was incredible, sweet and natural and soft all at the same time. As I followed her outside, a huge, pale-colored flower smacked into my face.

"Watch where you're going!" she scolded me. She straightened the flower. "These are my orchids. It takes a lot of work to make these guys bloom, you know. That's why I don't have many of them."

We walked together through her garden. There were flowers of every color of the rainbow. They came in clusters, growing out of different-sized planters. Some of them hadn't bloomed yet. Some of them had bloomed so big that they looked swollen in size. One of the flowers was bright blue. I didn't even know that flowers could be that shade of blue.

"This is really impressive," I told her. "Didn't you just move here this year?" She nodded. "How did you have time to do all of this?"

"The garden was much bigger at my old house," she explained. "We were able to move a lot of the flowers easily, though, since most of them are in pots. Some of them I had to regrow. But this..."

She came to a stop. I bumped into her, then I stopped too. I followed her gaze and looked up.

At the back corner of the garden was the most massive lemon tree I'd ever seen. It was bright green, all of the leaves fully spread out and facing upwards toward the sky. Lemons grew in enormous bushels all about the branches. They weren't the sad little greenish ones I saw at the market, either; they were huge, fat, and a happy daisy yellow color.

"This is my lemon tree," Polly announced with pride. Her eyes twinkled as she looked at it, as if it were her own child. "I grew it since I was a little kid in Eagle River. Biggest lemon tree you'd ever seen. When my parents told me we were moving, I refused to go with them unless they transplanted my tree."

I gawked at her. "You can do that? Transplant trees?"

"It's risky, and expensive, but yeah." Polly grinned. "You can, and I did. We had to pull it out of the ground and stick it on the back of a truck. When you transplant trees, you're not supposed to do it when they're bearing fruit. It puts a lot of stress on the tree. Almost every time, it ends up dying. But I couldn't just leave it where it was, you know? I mean, it's my tree. I feel like it's my responsibility, in a way. My parents were adamant on leaving it behind. I was more adamant on taking it with us. They kept telling me, 'I hope you know that there's a very slim chance of it actually surviving. Even if it survives the move, it probably won't be the same once we put it back in the ground. The roots might not grow again.'"

"Were you worried at all? That it would die?"

She pursed her lips. "No," she said thoughtfully. "I wasn't worried. I was just thinking about moving it. It would be a waste to think about what might happen afterward.

152

I didn't listen to my parents, I just kept fighting them on it until they gave in." She smiled, putting her hand up against the trunk of the lemon tree. She ran her fingers down the rough bark. "And I'm so glad I fought for this tree. Best thing I ever did."

"A lemon tree," I remarked. "Wouldn't you rather have an apple tree or something? Lemons are so…"

"Sour," she said. "Yes. Everyone immediately shrinks away from the taste of lemons because it's shocking, right? You don't expect any fruit to taste like that. But then when you take a sip of lemonade all of a sudden you remember why you love lemons; they're sweet, they're sour, they're everything that a fruit can be. That's what *makes* them the best fruit."

"I like your tree," I admitted. "It's very pretty."

"Very very." She pointed up at it. "You know, the ones on top are riper. I can't reach up there. Can you pick them for me?"

So I did. I climbed halfway up her fence and plucked all of the biggest lemons from the highest branches and she was waiting from the bottom to catch them in her arms when I tossed them down to her. She was beaming. I loved her smile. I loved the way she let all of her emotions show on her face like that.

"What are you going to do with all these, anyway?" I asked, detaching myself from the fence and jumping down to where she was standing.

Polly clicked her tongue at me, shaking her head. "You weren't listening at all," she told me, her arms cradling the fruits. "Making lemonade, of course."

"You can just buy lemonade at the store," I pointed out. "It'll probably taste better, anyway."

"You know I can't do that."

"Why not?"

"Think, Drew." Polly turned to face me. She was still holding the lemons in her arms;

there were so many that it was really a wonder how they all stayed there like that without falling. "Why would I want to make my own lemonade instead of buying it at the store?"

Because you don't do anything the normal way? "I don't know," I said instead.

And then, like lightning, I remembered:

"Preservatives. You hate fruit preservatives."

Polly grinned.

"So you *do* pay attention to me."

16

On Wallace's birthday, I picked up balloons at the convenience store before school. I didn't have enough money for the fancy kind so I just got two of the regular helium ones in green, Wallace's favorite color.

Brent and I met Wallace just outside the school gates. "Happy birthday!" we both shouted.

Brent had bought a cupcake for Wallace. While I tied the balloons to Wallace's backpack, Brent handed over the cupcake, still in the plastic box from the store.

"You guys didn't have to," Wallace said sheepishly. His face was glowing.

"What do you mean?" Brent said. "Of course we did. You're 15 now. You're officially an adult."

Wallace laughed. He opened his mouth to respond, but a different voice cut through the air behind us.

"Hey!"

We all turned around.

Polly was walking towards us. She was carrying a brown paper bag.

As soon as she reached us, she wrestled Wallace into a hug. "Happy birthday," she said. She pulled back. She reached into the bag and pulled out a single cupcake wrapped in foil.

"Here," she said, handing it to him. "I baked this just for you."

"You did?" Wallace examined it.

"Yup." Polly smiled at him. "I had to go to the store and get eggs and flour and stuff just so I could bake that cupcake, so enjoy it."

"At least you have more cupcakes at home, though," I said. "Like, the other ones."

She looked at me. "What do you mean?"

I frowned. "Well, you baked them in at least a dozen, didn't you? So don't you have more at home?"

Polly blinked. "No, I baked one."

"Didn't you have too much batter?"

157

"No, I made enough batter for one."

"Thanks, Polly," Wallace said.

"Don't mention it." Polly looked at me, poked me in the arm. "See you later."

I hadn't even noticed how quiet Brent had gotten until he piped back up again. "What was that?" he said. "How did she know it was your birthday?"

Wallace looked almost guilty, like he'd been caught doing something he wasn't supposed to. "Uh," he said. "I told her yesterday."

"You're friends with her too, now?"

"I don't know. We talk during class and stuff."

"Yeah, but you guys are like… you know." Brent made a little hand gesture. "Like, tight? She actually knows you well enough to bring you a cupcake?"

"I don't know," Wallace said again. "I don't think she really thinks about that kind of stuff, you know? She just does whatever she wants."

Wallace put both the cupcakes into his lunch bag gingerly. I watched Brent's face the whole time and I knew he was thinking exactly what I was thinking. Even though his cupcake was bigger and more neatly decorated, hers was strangely endearing in its ugliness. It was sloppy, frosting coming over the sides, and it had a little heart made of icing sitting on top.

He was thinking, *when did Polly Park start taking over our lives?*

And, yeah. I was sort of wondering the same thing. But I wasn't too bothered by it at all.

17

Brent made us all stay after Mathletes practice. He had a surprise for all of us. "I'll be back in, like, two minutes," Brent promised, a feverish grin plastered on his face. "Wait here, okay?"

He returned to the multi-purpose room exactly a minute and a half later. He was carrying a big cardboard box in both arms. It looked way too heavy for him; he was practically staggering with each step, but his eyes were glittering all the same.

"Alright," he said, dropping the box onto the stage. "Gather round, folks."

Brent opened up the box. He reached inside and pulled out a navy blue jacket. Across the front, 'Mathletes' was embroidered in red.

Jess was the first to run over. "No way." She grabbed another one from the box. "These turned out so cute!" she gushed, holding the jacket out in front of herself and admiring it front-and-back.

Brent was trying to play aloof, but his face was already starting to redden. "They're nice, right?"

"So nice," Jess agreed. "I'm trying it on."

Brent handed one to Wallace, then one to me. The jacket was unreasonably well-made. It was soft leather, but it was also thick and durable, the expensive kind. I glanced up at Brent, feeling almost guilty that he'd bought such a pricey gift for us.

Jess finished pulling the jacket on. "Oh my god," she said, "I love it." She turned to Brent. "It looks good, right?"

"Yup," he said faintly. "Yeah. Yup. Really good."

Jess smiled. She nudged Brent's shoulder. "You were right," she said. "Mathletes *is* the coolest."

18

Polly started calling me at night so I could help her with her essays.

"It's too hard," she complained. "Writing is just too subjective, you know? At least with science and math and history, there's always just one answer. Like, 'I got 5.' 'That's wrong.' 'Oh, okay, I'm wrong.' But with writing, it's like, 'I think this book is about revenge.' 'Yeah, maybe, but have you considered this?'"

She groaned on the other end of the line. I had my cell phone pressed against my ear in one hand, my laptop open on my lap with her essay pulled up for me to proofread. With my free hand, I scrolled slowly down the page, my eyes darting back and forth across the screen while I read.

"There are so many themes," Polly said. "How can there be so many themes in *one* book? It's exhausting. This is why I told you reading is the worst." She stopped for a moment. "Drew, are you even listening to me?"

"Shakespeare uses metaphor," I said.

"What?"

"You wrote, 'metaphor is used by Shakespeare to show how Macbeth is slowly beginning to lose his peace of mind.'"

"Okay. And?"

"It's supposed to be 'Shakespeare uses metaphor.' You're not supposed to use passive voice in response to literature."

"Oh my god," Polly said, "what's the *difference?*"

I shrugged, then realized quickly after that she couldn't see it. "I don't know, that's just how it is," I told her.

She went silent. I saw her go in and fix it on the document; over the phone I could hear her fingers pecking away at her keys.

I cleared my throat. "And, um. You spelled 'necessary' wrong."

Polly groaned loudly. "I quit," she said. "I quit everything."

"Don't quit," I said.

"I quit," she said again. "I mean, I was starting to have fun reading *Macbeth*. Now this is making me hate it. Do you even think it's good, Drew? Tell me honestly. Do you think it's a good essay?"

"...Yeah."

Polly made a sound that was somewhere between a laugh and a howl. "You are *such* a liar, it just amazes me."

"It has good parts," I insisted. "You have a strong argument. It's just, you know, your conventions could use just a little bit of work."

"You know, I think your sugarcoating is adorable."

If this was a face-to-face conversation, I was almost sure she'd be petting me on the head right now. I was glad she wasn't here to see the way my face flushed. "Okay," I said stupidly.

"I just don't understand how you could possibly like writing," she said. "It's so complicated. And it's so hard."

"It is complicated," I agreed. "But it's also... I don't know. It's almost like an outlet, you know? It's like, I've got all these words and ideas and stories just... just swirling around in my head aimlessly. Writing lets me put all of that down somewhere. It's... kind of therapeutic, in a way."

"I like listening to you talk about writing," she said. "You make it sound so poetic and beautiful."

"It is beautiful," I said.

"But you'd rather do math in college."

I deflated a little. "Well, yeah."

"So what's better about math?"

I didn't even have to think about it. "Job security," I said easily. "Money. Near-guaranteed success. Familiarity. Respect."

"You don't think people will respect you if you choose writing?"

"Everyone already sees me as a math person."

"Yeah, yeah, left-brained, logical, whatever." Polly snorted. "You sound ridiculous when you talk like that. Who cares how everyone sees you? What matters is how you see yourself, remember?"

I felt a sinking feeling in my chest. There was a strange spell of silence that fell upon us, and Polly must have sensed it.

"Don't worry," she said. "I'm not going to ask. I know you've still got no clue."

I said nothing. Slowly, I turned my gaze back to my laptop screen.

"You spelled 'receive' wrong."

"I thought it was 'I' before 'E' if it's after 'C'."

"'I' before 'E' *unless* after 'C'."

I could practically hear Polly grinning into the phone. Then more key-pecking. "See," she said, "this is exactly why you're my editor."

19

I would've completely forgotten about winter formal if not for the absolute chaos it wreaked upon Brent's mental state.

He was a mess. A jumbled-up, freckle-faced, wide-eyed, caffeine-fueled mess who had decided that he was going to ask Jess out to winter formal.

"So we blew it on Halloween," he said. "But this— *this* is a foolproof plan. For real." Brent turned to me and grabbed me by the shoulders. "But you have to be there for me, alright? You have to be there."

I still didn't quite get the whole formal proposal thing. It was some phenomenon that had sparked popularity years ago, and had become spiraled into the insane fad it was now. Guys got all spiffed up and made little posters with stupid puns on them, sang stupid songs, gave stupid flowers to their stupid victims, and finally proposed the stupid question: *Will you go to formal with me?*

But Brent was right about one thing. It was a foolproof plan. I'd almost never seen a girl decline a dance proposal from anyone. At the very least, it was a sure way to get the girl you liked to spend an entire night with you.

Wallace and I went to Brent's house after school to help him prepare. He had decided to go the traditional route, with a poster and a bouquet of flowers. He insisted it was because he didn't want to do anything too flashy. I speculated it was because he didn't have the guts to do anything more than the bare minimum.

When Brent went to go get art supplies, I turned to Wallace.

"What about you?" I asked him. "Do you have any girls you're planning on asking?"

Wallace reddened. "No," he said. His voice came out squeaky. "Um. Not really. Are you gonna ask Polly?"

My brain completely short-circuited. I hadn't even thought about it until then. I swallowed. "I'm… like, supposed to do that, aren't I?"

Wallace shrugged. "Well, you like her, don't you?"

Brent decided on a math pun for Jess's poster. We drew on the message in giant, shaky handwriting:

You + Me = Winter Formal?

It seemed way too simple to me. And it didn't reveal anything about Jess, her personality, or her interests; it was just a regurgitation of the fact that she was a Mathlete. It made me wonder if Brent even knew anything about Jess other than that she was good at math. I wondered if he *liked* anything about her other than that.

The entire time we worked on her poster, I was thinking about whether I should ask Polly. I knew she liked me. I knew I liked her too. The thing was, I hadn't been to a high school dance before. I hadn't even been planning to until Polly came along. Did she even like these sorts of things? Did she have school dances in Eagle River?

Even though I knew asking girls to dances worked almost every time, I also knew that Polly wasn't exactly the most conventional person to be on the receiving end of a proposal. I played out the possible scenarios in my head. In one, I did a poster just like Brent: *I would be very very happy if you went to winter formal with me.* I could almost picture her face looking at it, her eyebrows raised in surprise, lips pursed. The conversation would be unbearably awful.

Her: You made this poster just to ask me?

Me: Yup.

Her: Isn't that a little much?

Me: Yup.

Her: You did a pretty crappy job. You're really bad at arts and crafts, aren't you?

Me: Yup.

Her: You know you think way too much about this stuff?

Me: Yup.

In another scenario, I didn't make a poster at all. I didn't buy flowers or dress nice or anything. Just chickened out completely. I was sitting in class with her and she turned to face me.

Her: Are you going to ask me?

Me: Nope.

Her: You have any idea why?

Me: Nope.

Her: You really don't have any guts, huh?

Me: Nope.

Her: And nothing to say for yourself?

Me: Nope.

I couldn't tell which was worse— asking or not asking. Either way I could only imagine my attempts ending in failure. There really was no way to approach her about something like this. It seemed below her. More accurately, she seemed *above* all this, soaring high in the sky, so far up I could hardly make out the soles of her shoes from the ground.

At least things went exactly according to plan for Brent. He went up to Jess during lunch. She went absolutely nuts. When she hugged him he looked like he was two seconds away from passing out, though I was certain he'd deny that later.

Besides, I didn't think she had any particular interest in him. She was more interested in the flowers and the poster and all the turned heads in the cafeteria, just as Brent was more interested in her dark lipstick and quick answers during math competitions.

"Brent's poster was so cheesy," Polly whispered to me during English.

"Yeah," I said, a bit absently.

"Did you help make it?"

"Yeah."

"You couldn't think of anything better to write?" Polly snorted. "I mean, '*you plus me*', that's awful. If someone asked me out with a poster like that I'd laugh in their face."

"Yeah."

We sat in silence for a couple seconds, even though the noise in my head was anything

172

but quiet. I could almost feel her thinking, too, watching my expression to see how I'd reacted to that. I put on my best poker face. I was pretty good at that.

Then Polly spoke again.

"Hey," she said.

She poked me in the arm.

"Let's go to winter formal together. Yeah?"

The world around us melted away as I looked at her. All of my made-up scenarios were dying and fading on the spot, my brain finally slowing to a dead stop.

"Yeah," I said.

20

"I have to buy a yellow tie," I told my dad during dinner.

It was the first time I'd actively conversed with him in weeks. He looked up from his plate at me from across the table. Blinked twice. "Huh?"

"I have to buy a yellow tie." I cleared my throat, trying to sound nonchalant even though I knew I'd already failed. "Unless you have one already."

"You *have* to buy a yellow tie," he repeated. I nodded without hesitation. "What's the occasion?"

"I'm going to winter formal."

"Really," Dad said. "With who?"

"Wallace and Brent." Not *technically* a lie. I was learning things from Polly already.

"Any girls?"

"No." Well, maybe not.

"So then, who are you trying to impress?" Dad smiled a little. "Why do you need a yellow tie?"

I shrugged. "I like yellow," I said simply. I shoved a forkful of peas into my mouth. *It looks good on me.* "I've been wearing it more often lately."

"I don't have any yellow ties," Dad told me. "Nobody has yellow ties. Kind of an ugly color, don't you think?"

He chuckled. For some reason, it annoyed me more than anything. He wasn't helpful at all. Beyond that, he didn't understand anything that was going on in my life at all; or anything that was going on in my head, for that matter.

"I'll just go to the thrift store," I ground out between clenched teeth.

Now Dad's smile dropped. He definitely sensed my irritation. He quieted, his voice dropping lower as he said, "Everything alright?"

I forced a smile onto my own face.

175

"Yup," I said cheerily. "Everything's okay."

21

Polly loved the tie.

"You look nice," she said. She was wearing a yellow dress, too. My tie was mustard yellow; her outfit was a bright, more saturated shade. We didn't quite match. She didn't seem to care one bit. "Took my advice, didn't you?"

"I always take your advice."

She straightened my tie. "Yeah, you do."

Her hair was still down like it always was. In fact, it seemed a little messier than usual, as if she'd brushed it only half-heartedly today. She wasn't wearing makeup. She looked just as she did every other day of the week, like this was no special occasion for her.

"I have something for you," Polly sang. She pulled out a bushel of flowers. They were silky and white, with streaks of purple in the middle, and looked strangely familiar.

"Orchids," I realized, snapping my fingers. "These are the ones that hit me in the face."

Polly looked offended. "No, you hit *them* with your face," she corrected me. "But, yes, these are my orchids."

I looked down and realized that she was already wearing some of the orchids on her wrist. "Wait," I said. "You made a corsage and boutonniere out of them?"

Her lips quirked up as she tried to suppress a grin. "Stand still, let me pin it on you."

So I stood still while Polly slid the pin through my left lapel. It was like she was attaching part of herself to me, latching onto my heart.

"It looks good," she told me, stepping back. Then she looped her arm through mine. "Let's head inside."

The dance was held in the gym. We were supposed to meet Wallace, Brent, and Jess by the doors. It immediately became clear that that wasn't quite possible anymore, with the room packed door-to-door with kids, all

178

surging past each other aimlessly. The lights were blinding, all different colors, shooting out in every direction. Other than that, the gym was shrouded in inky blue darkness.

Polly darted out into the crowd. I followed after her as closely as I could, bumping into countless shoulders to keep up with her. She didn't slow down or wait for me, so it was near impossible to keep up with her.

"This place is a madhouse," she said. "What even *is* this music? It's awful."

It was hardly music. All I could hear was bass screaming from the speakers, overlayed by a trap beat. "Yeah," I said.

"Where are Brent and Jess?"

"I don't know."

"Where's Wallace?"

"Probably with Brent and Jess."

"It's so hard to find anyone in here," she said, squinting as she peered back and forth. Then she glanced out at the crowd, at how everyone was moving but there was a gaping hole in the center of the dance floor. She frowned. "Why's nobody dancing?"

"People don't dance at school dances."

She barked out a laugh. "Ha, ha. Funny."

"I wasn't joking."

Now she looked alarmed. She whipped around to look at me. "Wait, seriously?" she said. "It's called a school *dance*. What's the point of coming here if you're not going to dance?"

I shrugged. "It's embarrassing," I suggested.

"What about it?"

"Being in front of everyone and just like— I don't know. It makes you look stupid, I guess. Makes you look vulnerable. It's scary."

Polly stared at me. I saw her jaw set, and my heart dropped into my shoes. I knew what she had made up her mind to do, but that didn't stop me from praying that for once in her life she would hold back.

"Polly," I started.

And then she grabbed my wrist and started dragging me right into the middle of the dance floor.

"Polly!" I shrilled. I couldn't keep my cool anymore, not when everyone was turned and watching us standing there alone in the center of the gym while the music blasted. "What are you doing?!"

"Dance with me," she said.

I glanced nervously at the crowd, at all of the blurred faces that were staring at us. "No."

"Dance with me," she said again.

"No."

Polly held my gaze for a long moment.

"Fine," she said. And then she started to move.

I swear to god, I've never seen a worse dancer.

And I swear to god, I've never seen anyone dance as freely as she did.

Her arms swooped in long, eagle-like motions around herself. She took these weird

181

little steps in a circle, twirling around so that she looked almost like she was flying. All around us, I could hear the conversations quieting as more people turned to look.

My face was burning. "Polly," I said again. "Polly."

She wasn't stopping. "Yes?"

"Everyone's watching."

"I know."

"Polly."

She still didn't stop. But for the third time, she looked at me and said, "Dance with me."

And, well. I really never had a choice to begin with when I was around her.

So I danced.

I danced and the lights disappeared and the gym disappeared and all the people were suddenly gone. I found myself in a room made of pure white, and in it only she stood, in her dress made of sunshine and her endless black eyes staring into my soul.

The air seemed lighter when I was moving through it. Gravity was gone. My feet lifted

182

off the ground and we were soaring together.

Everything that had once bound us to the earth was suddenly forgotten. I only knew her and her yellow dress and her name. Polly Park. Polly Park. Polly Park. I lived inside my own head, but this was how she lived. Always flying, always free.

I wasn't thinking about how stupid I looked, even though I'm sure I did look stupid. But all I could feel was the music, how my feet felt like they were floating, and I let myself disappear.

Then I felt her poking my arm the way she always did.

"Hey," she said.

I blinked myself back to reality. We were back in the crowded gym, standing in the middle of the room.

"Brent and Jess," she told me. "I see them. Come with me."

She yanked me back into the swarm of students and away from the dance floor.

Once again I bumped into shoulder after shoulder, mumbling apologies that got lost in the blaring music.

Brent and Jess were standing by the entrance. Like Polly and I, they'd come in matching colors, both of them wearing dark red and black. The difference was that the shade of maroon on Brent's tie actually matched Jess's dress. Jess's skirt went down to her ankles, unlike Polly's, which only reached her knees. Their corsage and boutonniere were made up of roses and had clearly been professionally done.

Brent was muttering something into Jess's ear that must have been insanely funny by the way she cackled laughing. She grinned when she saw us. "Hey!"

Brent looked happier than I'd seen him in a long time. Not just fake-happy, either. Real happy. He was beaming too. "Hey," he said, a perfect mirror of Jess's voice.

"Hi," I said.

"What have you two been doing since you got here?" Polly asked.

Jess shrugged. "Just hanging out."

I glanced around. "Where's Wallace?"

Brent blinked. He looked around too. "Huh," he said. "He was with us earlier. He must've slipped away."

I instantly knew something was wrong. Wallace wouldn't just *slip away* to go off on his own. He needed people to latch onto at these sorts of events.

"You lost him?" I accused Brent.

Brent frowned. "What is he, a dog or something? I'm not his babysitter, Drew. He's not my responsibility."

My jaw dropped. "He's our *friend*," I said. "You're not supposed to leave him alone."

"Dude, he's fine. Relax." I noticed Brent's arm was linked tightly around Jess's. "He probably just went to the bathroom or something."

"Drew," Polly said. "Come on, let's go."

She was tugging at my arm. I frowned.
"But—"

"Come *on.*"

I glanced back at Brent and Jess. Jess had gone back to giggling hysterically, and Brent had taken that dumb grin up again.

My blood was boiling with annoyance. I turned away and followed Polly.

"Where are we going?"

"To find Wallace," Polly said.

We left the gym. Cool air rushed into my face. As we walked further away, the music became more distant, sounding almost like it was underwater. Polly jogged around the outside of the gym, circling it.

"Think he's in the locker room?" she asked as we walked by it.

"They close the locker rooms during these kinds of events," I told her. We passed the closed door. Then I spotted the bathroom. "Maybe he's in there."

Polly skipped ahead. I had to speed up to keep her pace, until I was practically running. My feet were aching in my dress shoes.

She practically kicked open the door. I grabbed her by the arm. "Polly!" I yelped.

She stopped, turning around. "What?"

"This is the boy's bathroom." My face was burning. "There could be people inside."

Polly looked at me. She gave a sort of half-shrug before striding into the bathroom. Of course she didn't care.

"Wallace?" she called out loudly. "Are you in here?"

She came to a sudden stop. I stopped behind her. Then I looked.

Wallace was sitting with his back against the tile wall, his legs curled up to his chest. His eyes were red and puffy around the edges. When he looked up and saw us, he instantly shrank back, wiping his cheeks furiously with his palms and trying for a smile.

"Hi," Wallace croaked. "What are you two doing in here?"

187

Polly was staring down at him. "We came looking for you."

"Oh." He cleared his throat. "Well, you guys can leave. I'm just, uh... just chilling out."

I raised my eyebrows. "On the bathroom floor?"

Wallace laughed, but it sounded like it was being dragged out of him. His fingers nervously drummed against his knees.

"You know, the dance is a lot more fun in the gym," Polly said. "Why don't you come back with us?"

He shook his head. "No, no, I can't do that." His eyes were closed.

"Why not?"

"I just... I don't do great, at things like this." Wallace inhaled, taking a shaky, shallow breath. "I mean, there are so many people, and everyone's with someone else and I just... I can't stand it. I can't breathe when I'm all alone in there and everyone else is just, you know."

"You won't be alone," Polly told him. "We'll be with you."

"Yeah, but you two are like." Wallace made an awkwardly placed hand motion. "Together. Just like Brent and Jess. Together. You know?"

"Is this about being with someone?" Polly said, tilting her head curiously "Wallace, we can get you with a girl."

"No!" Wallace said, too quickly. He winced at the sound of his own voice. "I mean, it's not about being with a girl, it's— it's the fact that I *can't* be with a girl."

"Why not?"

"Because I don't *like girls!*"

Wallace's eyes widened in shock, as if he was only just registering now what he'd said. His fingers tightened around his dress pants. He seemed to shrink even smaller against the bathroom wall.

"Oh," he stammered out. "I— I didn't mean to— I mean, I don't— I, um... I'm sorry. Uh. Sorry."

"Hey," Polly said. Her voice was surprisingly steady. When I looked at her, her face hadn't changed. "Why are you sorry?"

"Because I'm..." Wallace swallowed. He hugged his legs closer to his chest. "You know. I just... I wish I could, you know? Just be normal, like everyone else."

"Wallace Morton," Polly said slowly. "You are not like anyone else in the world and that's what makes you so freaking incredible."

Wallace's ears turned pink. He squeaked a bit, suddenly incapable of forming words.

"If you don't want to go back," I said, "you don't have to."

"My mom's coming to pick me up soon," he told us. "So you two can just leave now." He laughed shakily. "I'm okay."

"We'll walk you to the parking lot and wait for her to come," I offered.

Wallace looked up at me, eyes shining. He sucked in a breath that disappeared into a hiccup. "But you'll miss the rest of the dance."

"Who cares about the stupid dance?" Polly said. "Come here."

She extended her hand. Wallace took it and she helped him to his feet.

None of us said anything as we walked out of the bathroom and into the cold night. Wallace wouldn't look at me. His head was bowed.

I nudged him with my shoulder. "Have you told anyone?"

He shook his head. "No," he murmured. He closed his eyes. "I think about it all the time, but I could hardly even say it out loud. It's hard to admit to myself, you know? It makes me feel... I dunno, like some sort of alien in my own skin. It's— it's terrifying."

Polly had fallen silent on his other side. We reached the empty parking lot and came to a stop in front of the curb.

Then Polly lifted her face up to the sky.

191

"Wallace Morton is gay and I love him!" she shouted at the top of her lungs.

Wallace squawked, eyes huge. "What are you doing?!" he demanded.

For a second I was terrified, gawking at her in disbelief. What *was* she doing? What if he wasn't ready to tell the whole world he was gay?

But then she locked eyes with me, and I saw that she had a peculiar gleam in her eye. Beside me, I noticed that Wallace was trying to keep his face serious, but he was struggling to suppress the smile that was inevitably spreading across his face.

I looked around us and saw that the parking lot was deserted. Aside from ourselves, there wasn't a single person within earshot. And I realized.

Polly wasn't saying it because she wanted the world to hear it. She wanted *him* to hear it.

So I took a deep breath.

"Wallace Morton is gay and I love him!" I yelled as loud as I could.

Wallace couldn't hide his smile anymore. He burst out laughing now. He was laughing so hard that tears were welling up in his eyes. He laughed and laughed and laughed, doubling over, unable to stop himself.

"Go on," said Polly. She was beaming too. She poked him in the shoulder. "Say it."

Wallace wiped the tears away from his eyes, grinning from ear to ear. He straightened, raising his face to the empty night sky.

"I'm gay, and I love myself!" he screamed, laughing the whole way through.

Wallace was suddenly standing straighter than ever before. I never noticed until that moment just how tall he was. He seemed as big as a mountain, his chest puffed out and his shoulders squared. He was confident. He was liberated. Nothing was making him small anymore. He was just getting bigger, bigger, and bigger.

He was still smiling uncontrollably by the time his mom pulled up to the curb.

"Bye, Polly," he said. "Bye, Drew."

"Bye," we both said.

Wallace started off towards his car. Then he stopped suddenly.

He turned back around, grabbed both of us, pulled both of us into a hug.

"Thank you," he said.

I'd never seen him so happy. He pulled away and got into his car; we watched it drive away, disappearing into the empty, silent street.

Polly started taking a few steps forward. There wasn't really anywhere to go, but she just walked out onto the road. There were no cars or people around. Just the two of us, alone. I found myself following after her into the street.

"You're amazing," I told her.

Polly looked at me. She was smiling, kind of secretive. "Yeah?"

"Yeah."

"How so?"

"I've known Wallace since middle school,"
I said. "In all that time, I've never seen him so
happy. He's always been sort of closed off,
and just really… unsure, you know? But, I
mean, look what you did to him. He was
smiling like… like… I don't even know. He
was smiling like he didn't have a care in the
world. You did that, Polly."

Crickets were chirping almost soundlessly
in the quiet night. Polly's face was dark in the
shadows, but I saw something in her eyes
change.

"I like when you do that," she said.

"What?"

"Give me all the credit."

"You deserve it," I said. "You're kind of
like a miracle."

Polly grinned. She took a step closer to me.
"I really like your tie."

"You said that already."

"I know." Another step. "I just wanted to
say it again."

"Yeah? Because it's yellow?"

"Right, because it's yellow. And because it looks nice with your face."

She took one more step. Now she was standing so close that I had to crane my neck to look down at her. I could see every detail of her face up close like this. Her black eyes weren't quite black at all; they were still astoundingly dark-colored, but with the street lamps illuminating her face I could see faint flecks of warm brown in her irises. She had unruly, hairy eyebrows, and it was a bit hard to tell where they began and ended. Her dry lips were pressed into a firm, straight line. Distantly, I remembered my very first observations of her appearance. *There was nothing striking about her.* What an idiot I'd been. Everything about her was striking. Every little thing, from her so-close-but-not-quite-black eyes to her chapped lips. She stared up at me.

"I think you're very cute, you know," she said.

My mouth suddenly felt dry. "Very very?" My voice came out barely above a whisper.

"Very very."

In the silence of the street, I could still hear the music from the gym. It had been ear-shatteringly loud when we were on the dance floor. Now that we were far away, the music was duller and softer. A muted, distant hum. I listened as the song eased into a much slower, gentler beat.

Polly took my hand in hers. "Drew Hartford, will you dance with me?" she asked.

"Yeah," I said.

And we were dancing. Except it wasn't anything like before. She grabbed my other hand, and then placed both my hands around her waist. Her yellow dress was soft under my fingertips.

She pulled me a bit closer to her. Placed her hands on my shoulders. Her touch was warm; I melted into it. She stood up on her tiptoes and leaned forward until her head rested against my collarbone. Her eyes were closed.

We slow danced together like that, neither of us saying a word. We just danced, and it was just me and her in the middle of the empty parking lot, and nothing else in the world mattered in that moment.

22

Just before I went to bed that night, I unpinned Polly's orchid boutonniere and placed it on the desk next to my bed.

I had decided I would keep it forever. It wasn't just a bunch of flowers to me; it was a piece of her that she'd pinned onto a piece of me, so now it was something new entirely, something fragile and meaningful all the same. I stared at the clipped orchids in the dark until my eyelids grew too heavy and I finally let them slide shut.

I went to sleep that night thinking about the color yellow.

I wondered why Polly loved that color so much. I saw her yellow dress and how it folded under my fingers around her waist.

Her voice sang in my head. *Think, Drew. Why do I like the color yellow?*

I saw her skipping down the sidewalk with arms full of Halloween candy, her bumble bee skirt flying behind her as she ran.

Then she was standing in her backyard, her arms overflowing with lemons as she watched me pluck more from her tree.

And she was dancing with me in the dark, her head on my shoulder, her dress swaying silently back and forth as we rocked in the street.

I thought of her smile, free and untethered by anyone or anything in the world. She was open. She felt every emotion to its full extent, without any hiding or shying away. When she smiled, she glowed like the sun.

I understood now just why she liked the color yellow so much. And it was because she *was* the color yellow.

23

Brent slammed his tray down so hard that the entire lunch table shook. Beside me, Wallace yelped in alarm, diving forward to protect his own tray from falling.

"I did it," Brent announced proudly. He sat down. A huge grin was plastered across his face.

I stared at him. "Okay."

Wallace fed into it. "What did you do?"

Brent grinned. He leaned back in his seat, casually placing his hands behind his neck.

"I walked Jess home last night, after the dance," Brent said. "And when we got to her porch, she kissed me. I kissed her. We kissed."

The word "kissed" was beginning to sound gross to me. "Are you serious?" I asked.

"Serious as serious gets," Brent said confidently. "We're dating. Officially." He pursed his lips, smug, and enunciated: "Boyfriend-and-girlfriend."

I found it strange the way he said that. Like suddenly everything was different between them, just because they decided to use those words to describe their relationship.

Polly wasn't my girlfriend. At least, I didn't think she was. Well, then again, I'd never had a relationship with anybody that was quite like the relationship I shared with her. Maybe she was my girlfriend and just didn't want to call it that; maybe she was already calling it that and I just didn't know. Did that make me her boyfriend? I kind of liked the sound of that. Me, Drew Hartford, Polly Park's boyfriend. I wondered if that was what she thought of me. There was no way of telling.

I stayed with Polly at Literature Society after school that day. She was elated. I was surprised to find that we were among the only few students who came into the classroom to attend.

"This is a very small club," I whispered to her as I sat down next to her.

"Very very," she hummed.

Mrs. Pruitt smiled and took a seat across from me. "Mr. Hartford," she said. "You're going to join us today?"

"Yeah." I glanced at Polly, who grinned back at me. "Polly's told me a lot of good things about the club."

"Well, she's told me a lot of good things about you," Mrs. Pruitt told me. Polly nodded sagely. "I'm excited to see that you're extending your interests in English outside of class."

While everyone shared the narratives they'd written during a creative session from the previous meeting, Mrs. Pruitt came by my desk and handed me a piece of paper and a pencil.

"Why don't you write yours now?" she suggested. "You can turn it in to me after the meeting."

The prompt was extremely vague, which threw me off. Mrs. Pruitt insisted that was the best way to tap deep into your most creative thoughts. *Write a narrative that reveals*

203

something about your life right now. The only guideline was to keep it short— three hundred words or less.

Something about my life right now. I thought hard.

Next to me, Polly was reading her own narrative. I studied her face as she read aloud to the group, her brow knit with focus while she scanned her paper.

I wrote and tuned out everyone else while they read theirs. Through the entire meeting I just wrote and wrote and I didn't hear or see anything else. Just words on paper. Words and words and words. I lost myself in them.

It was strangely therapeutic, watching each word go from my brain to my hand to the paper, building until they filled up the page. It felt almost like cleaning out my head, making something beautiful out of all my meaningless thoughts.

I finished just as Mrs. Pruitt ended the club meeting.

"I'll see you all at our next meeting," she said. "That'll be next month. Have a great day, everyone."

Polly nudged me with her elbow. "You zoned out while I read mine," she said. "You didn't hear any of it, did you?"

"Sorry." I held up my paper. "I finished mine, though."

"Boo," she said. I could tell she wasn't actually bothered much, just playing around. "I hope you know that if you ever try to read yours to me, I won't have any of it. I'm just gonna tune you out, too."

Polly waited for me while I handed my narrative in to Mrs. Pruitt, who took it from me with a huge smile. "I'm excited to read it," Mrs. Pruitt told me. "Did you enjoy the meeting?"

"Yeah," I admitted truthfully. "I really did."

"You were quite absorbed in your writing," she remarked with a short laugh.

I shrugged. "I guess I had a lot to say."

205

"I hope to see you at our next meeting?"

I nodded. She told me "have a good day" and I said it back, like any nice boy would. When I turned, Polly was at my side, poking me in the arm.

"Hey," she said.

"Hey," I said. Then I said, "Thanks for bringing me here, Polly. This was really fun."

"Well, we can talk about that later," she told me. "Right now you better get going." Polly tapped her wristwatch with an impish grin. "Tick tock, right?"

I frowned. Blinked. "What do you mean?"

"Mathletes."

The world slowed down before coming to a dead stop. My eyes widened.

I turned and bolted out of the classroom, leaving Polly snickering inside. "See you tomorrow!" I heard her calling after me.

I tore down the hallway as fast as my legs could take me, sprinting towards the multi-purpose room. How could I have forgotten about Mathletes? Stupid!

By the time I reached it, I was practically gasping for breath. I stumbled into the doors and clumsily made my way down to the stage.

Brent, Wallace, and Jess were standing there. They all stared at me as I walked up.

"Sorry," I forced out between pants. "Sorry. What'd I miss?"

"We haven't even started," Wallace said.

Jess was giggling. I blinked dumbly.

"Oh," I said.

Then I realized something. I wasn't late. That meant Polly was right: I *could* go to Literature Society and Mathletes practice.

"Oh," I said again.

And I was smiling.

24

What We See While We're Falling
a narrative by Drew Hartford

I tend to run places instead of taking my time.
It's a bad habit of mine. If I chose to walk instead,
I'd have a much easier time maintaining my
balance. But I keep on running, because I'm
scared of what might happen if I slow down.

The other day I tripped over my own feet. I
pitched forward and I fell, but I didn't hit the
ground.

I found myself in an abyss that never ended.
Free-falling through the air, my arms flailing,
tumbling over myself, waiting for the ground to
rush up and crush me from below, except it never
did. I just fell.

While I was falling I tried to make sense of what
was going on around me. The thing is, you're so
disoriented, spinning around in midair with the
world rushing past you so fast that you can
hardly make out anything. But I'll tell you what I

saw while I was plummeting through the sky in that senseless blur.

I saw a fire, eating up everything in its path. I saw a street winding up and down and in every possible direction. I saw eagles that were soaring sideways. I saw colors, I saw yellow, I saw people and stars and faces and cars all spanned out before me.

We are all just stars, falling through space towards Earth. I fell, and I fall, and I'm falling. The ground still hasn't come.

If I walked this never would have happened. But I think I'll just enjoy the view while I'm here.

It's not as bad as you think.

25

I told Polly I was able to make Literature Society and Mathletes practice. She rolled her eyes at me.

"Duh," she said, "I literally told you that."

"Yeah. I should probably just start trusting you more often. You're always right."

"I *know*, I'm always right." She was grinning. "How's Mathletes practice going, anyway? Should I pay you another visit at the next one?"

"Don't bother. It's as boring as ever."

"How long are you guys going to keep those posters up around the school?" Polly asked. "They've been up since September, haven't they?

I nodded. "We're probably just gonna leave them up in hopes that by some miracle we'll get a new recruit out of it."

She tilted her head at me. "Does anyone even try out for the team?"

"We have open tryouts, but no one's come," I explained to her.

The girl sitting in the desk in front of me turned around suddenly. Nora Kermani. She was frowning. "You're talking about Mathletes, right?"

I blinked. "Yeah," I said. "Are you interested in trying out for the team?"

Nora looked at me with a quizzical expression on her face.

"I already did," she said.

26

"You didn't tell us."

Brent looked at me from across the lunch table. "Huh?"

Wallace was turning and looking at me too now. I kept my gaze fixed on Brent's face. "You didn't tell us," I repeat ed. "About Nora. You said nobody tried out for the team."

Wallace boggled. "Wait, *what?*" he spluttered. "Nora tried out for Mathletes?"

Brent looked unfazed. "Who told you that?"

"She did. During class."

"Nora tried out for Mathletes?" Wallace repeated, looking back and forth between Brent and I.

I didn't say anything. My lips were pressed in a tight straight line. I waited for Brent to speak.

He shrugged simply. "It just happened, like, last week," he said. "It wasn't a big deal or anything. We just met after school and I timed her while she did a few problems. She was too slow. I told her no."

Wallace's jaw dropped. "But we only have four members," Wallace said. "We could've still taken her."

"Trust me on this one," Brent told him. "Nora's like a snail, I swear. She took, like, two entire minutes just doing a single long division problem with polynomials. She's not even in Pre-Calc. She's in Geometry."

Wallace deflated. I could tell he was still skeptical about it, but he dropped it. "Okay," he said.

Brent glanced at me. "Why do you look so upset?"

"You said we didn't have any tryouts," I gritted out. "You lied."

He said nothing, pursing his lips. "I don't get why that's such a big deal to you," he said finally. "You lie all the time."

The bell rang. Brent got up and left. I turned to Wallace.

"What's he talking about?" I demanded.

"I don't know," Wallace said quickly. He walked away too, disappearing into the crowd of students rushing past to get to their last class. I stared after him.

I had a strange feeling that he did know.

27

A man in a cerulean blazer was pointing a gun at me, glowering from behind clunky glasses frames. Above his head was the word *Extermination*, printed in solid gold lettering.

"Extermination," Polly declared from behind the poster. She lowered the paper and peered at me over it. "The movie comes out today."

"I thought that movie came out, like, three years ago," I said.

"That was the first movie," she corrected me. "This is the sequel. Extermination Ultimate."

I took the poster from her. "Where'd you get this thing?"

"At the movie theater. I was walking by yesterday and they were selling them for promotion."

I laughed. "You like spy movies?"

"No, I *hate* spy movies," Polly said. "I *love* Extermination. Extermination is like its own genre. It's not like any other spy film you've ever seen. It's, like, ninety percent satire."

"I didn't know you appreciated satire."

"Drew, satire is literally just making fun of people. Who doesn't love making fun of people?"

I opened my mouth to respond to that, but she didn't give me the chance. She took the poster back from me. "We're going to watch it after school today."

"I haven't even watched the first one."

"You don't have to watch the first one. You know what?" She snapped her fingers. Pointed at me. "I've got the most brilliant idea, Drew. Meet me at the plaza at 5 tonight, okay? I can fill you in on everything that happened in the first movie."

"Okay," I said.

"Okay," she said. "Cool."

"Cool."

It didn't even occur to me until I got home that she'd asked me out on a date.

That *was* what you called it, right? Yeah.
Sure, we were together a lot. We'd been out
alone before. It wasn't Brent, or Wallace, or
my dad, or anyone else I was spending my
time with— it was her. In that sense, she had
sort of become my best friend. Even when
we'd gone to winter formal together, that
hadn't been a *date.* It was just another outing,
just like trick-or-treating on Halloween,
sneaking off to the book fair, walking in her
garden, only in front of other people.

But this was different. Way different. Two
people going to dinner and the movies was
definitely a date, I was convinced. If we were
just going to see a movie, that was one thing,
but *dinner*— that sealed the deal.

But we weren't even boyfriend-and-
girlfriend yet. Wasn't dating against the rules
unless you were boyfriend-and-girlfriend? Or
had I messed up the order? Maybe you were
supposed to go on a few dates first, and *then*
you became boyfriend-and-girlfriend.

How was that stuff even decided, anyway? Did I have to ask her for permission? *Hey, Polly, so we've been hanging out a lot now. I kinda like you a lot. Can I be your boyfriend? Like, officially?*

All those conversations were beginning to sound so stupid in my head. Just the word "like" was becoming stupid to me. Before, I'd been perfectly content with the idea that Polly and I *liked* each other. Now it felt like a vast understatement. How was a word that was used to describe middle school crushes possibly sum up the way I felt about her?

I didn't like Polly. When I was around her, I was scared out of my mind. Whenever Polly opened her mouth to speak, I froze up, turning into a sailor in a hurricane — completely stunned, helpless, abandoning the rational voice at the back of my head that insisted I shouldn't worry, I knew how to swim. But the problem was I'd only ever learned to swim in calm, shallow waters, and so now that I was thrown into the middle of a raging whirlpool, there was no telling whether I'd sink or float. Nothing could prepare me for the enigma that was Polly Park and her strange, mysterious mind.

And despite all this, I was more thrilled than anything to have become a tiny speck in Polly's universe. Her simultaneous brashness and authenticity were fascinating to me. I was drawn to her like a moth to light. I wanted nothing more than to be in her presence in every waking moment of my life, her presence which was so alienating and yet so real.

I tried sorting my life into two segments: Before and After. The first segment being my life before Polly came into my life, the second being after she arrived.

BEFORE
Nothing.
AFTER
Everything.

She was everywhere. She was there when I closed my eyes, when I dreamt, when I woke up in the morning, when I walked to school in the rain. She was always in my thoughts, perpetually on my mind. She'd become a part of me.

I didn't like her, because I was in love with her.

I was in love with Polly Park.

Now that was one thing I was sure of.

As soon as I got home, I was manic. I brushed my teeth ten times and then flossed so aggressively that my gums started to bleed. So then I spent another ten minutes washing my mouth out with water and trying to get the bleeding to stop. I scraped my tongue. I combed my hair back behind my ears and styled it with my mom's old hairspray.

Dad peered into the bathroom while I was staring into the mirror, obsessing feverishly over my part. "Hey," he said. I ignored him. "What are you doing?"

"Getting ready."

"For what?"

"I'm going to the movies."

"With who?"

"Brent," I lied.

"Oh."

"Yeah."

I waited for him to slip away again before returning my attention to the mirror.

I locked eyes with my reflection once more. Even with his hair styled, he was the same awful creature. I forced a smile onto my face and stared at myself for a few moments.

"Don't screw this up," I said, jabbing a finger at the boy in the mirror.

I dressed in my nicest shirt and tucked it in, a liberty I almost never had the time to take. I was pulling my socks on in my bedroom when suddenly I heard a laugh coming from downstairs.

I frowned, stopping with my sock around my ankle. That must have been my imagination. But then I heard my dad's voice, talking, muffled behind my bedroom door.

And then I heard her voice.

221

My stomach sank. I yanked my remaining sock on and threw the door open, stumbling down the stairs. *Please, no. Please, no. Anything but this.*

I skidded into the living room, horrified. Sure enough, Dad was standing beside the front door, and Polly was standing in the doorway.

"Dad," I said loudly.

I was kind of surprised that I said his name first and not hers. It was sort of just my knee-jerk reaction, just to break up whatever conversation they were having in my doorway, but part of me wondered why I didn't say her name.

Dad turned around. He was smiling. "Hey," he said. His hands were in his pockets and he was leaning against the side of the door. "I was just talking with your friend Polly."

He gave me a sort of strange look. His eyes were saying, *I didn't even know you* had *a friend named Polly.*

I tried to send him a message with my own eyes. *Please go away right now or I'm going to have an aneurysm.* It was hard to get that message across with a fake polite smile plastered across my face.

It was hopeless. I abandoned the cause entirely, turning to Polly instead. "Hi," I said to her. "Um, I thought we were meeting there."

"I know," she said. "I wanted to surprise you. Surprise."

"If you want, you can step inside," Dad offered to Polly. "I'm sure Drew would be happy to show you around the house."

"Actually," I cut in quickly, "we were just about to get going."

Polly stared at me as I wheeled her out the door, stepping into my shoes.

"Bye, Dad," I called.

Dad stopped me. He grabbed me by the arm and looked at me skeptically.

"So you're not meeting Brent, I'm guessing?" He said it like a joke, probably because he didn't want to scold me when Polly was still here, watching. I couldn't look him in the eye. I stopped while Polly walked down the porch steps to wait for me, giving us space.

Dad's smile faded as soon as she left us alone. "Drew," he said, kind of cross. "You didn't tell me you had a girlfriend."

I didn't object with that word, *girlfriend.* I just swallowed. My throat felt tight. I shrugged.

"Listen, Drew," Dad said. "I know we don't talk a whole lot, but you can tell me about this kind of stuff. You know that, right?"

"I'm *fine*, Dad," I insisted. I glanced nervously back at Polly, who was examining her sneakers. "I'll see you later, okay?"

Dad pursed his lips. "Alright," he said. "We'll talk about this later."

I turned away from him and joined Polly on the sidewalk. I heard him close the door behind me.

"Sorry about that," I said. "Let's get going."

Polly blinked. She looked at the car in the driveway, then looked at me. "Do you have your license?"

"I have my permit."

"So are you gonna drive us?"

I looked at her, skeptical. "Polly, that's illegal."

"Who shoved a stick up your butt?" she snorted. "Sophomores drive each other around all the time. It's just down the street."

"So we can walk." I started down the street before she could object. She trailed after me.

"You do *know* how to drive, right?"

"Yeah." I kicked absently at a rock on the sidewalk. "I just... don't like to."

Polly grew quiet, sensing my discomfort. She cleared her throat. She looked around herself, observing my neighborhood.

"Your dad is really nice," she said.

I didn't say anything. More discomfort, which she recognized almost instantly.

"So, anyway." Polly locked eyes with me and wagged a finger in my face. "The first Extermination movie."

I learned pretty quickly that her summary was much too scattered to follow clearly. She relayed every single plot detail to me, even taking the opportunity to include quotes here and there. She made sure to do her character voices, too. It turned out Polly had a breadth of different accents up her sleeve, and she put all of them on display for me: Welsh, cockney, Irish, Australian. There were ones I'd never even heard before, though I had a strange feeling that it might have just been her faulty impersonation.

As I listened to her, I found that I was more entertained by her mannerisms and storytelling than what she was actually saying. At one point the plot got too complicated and I became completely lost, nodding on senselessly while she rambled on.

"How do you remember all of this?" I asked her.

"I don't," she admitted. She grinned deviously. "I'm making it up in all the places that I forgot."

She finished by the time we reached the plaza. If anything, I was more confused about the film's premise than I'd been before she told me about it. But I was content anyway. I always seemed to be when I was with her.

"Let's eat here!" Polly said excitedly. She dragged me towards Chippies, a Western restaurant. "This is my favorite place."

We sat outside on the patio. I absolutely *hated* everything about Chippies. I hated how all their decor was supposed to be rustic-looking, but was actually just old and dirty. I hated how their chairs squeaked when you sat in them. I hated how they drowned all of their food in salt.

Of course, I didn't say any of this to her. I just ordered and sat down in a squeaky chair across from her and shoveled my meal into

227

my mouth without complaint, trying my best not to taste it.

We shared sweet potato fries. At least, 'sharing' was what *Polly* called it. We split the cost, but she ended up demolishing the entire tray. I didn't care.

"You eat like a bird," she criticized me. "All you do is peck at your food, you know? No wonder you're so skinny."

I snorted. "You sound like my mom."

Polly quieted. She bit into a fry. Her eyes surveyed the sky, and I could see that she was thinking. Then she turned to me.

"Tell me about her," she said.

That surprised me. Most people froze up every time my mom came into the conversation. It was like they considered it taboo to talk about. Probably because it went strictly against rule two. So when Polly just looked me in the eye and folded her arms across the table and *listened,* I couldn't help but stare at her in awe.

And of course, I obeyed.

228

"I was a lot closer to her than my dad," I told her. I picked up one of the fries and put it in my mouth. Still salty. I swallowed it. "Her name was Diane. She was really pretty… she always used to read to me. Like, you know *Dorian Gray?* She read that to me as a bedtime story when I was back in grade school. Sometimes I think that's why I like writing so much. When my mom read, it was like she brought the words to life."

I waited for Polly to talk. She didn't. She just stared at me, hanging onto every word, nodding. So I just kept talking.

"She always listened to rock music," I recalled. "Not just the soft, pretty kind, either. She was into hard rock, punk rock, metal… sometimes it even sounded like screamo. She would just blast it on full volume whenever we were in the house. One time a neighbor actually had to call to have her turn it down." I smiled. That was something I hadn't thought about in a while. "Her favorite color was blue. Dark, royal blue, like… like the blue you see at the very bottom of the ocean. She was awful at cooking. She hated the taste of alcohol. She loved looking at the stars."

I glanced at Polly. "We used to go stargazing all the time," I told her. "But it's hard to find places to look at them, you know?"

Polly's eyes were shining. "Why?"

"You can only see them from high up." I closed my eyes, trying to imagine how they looked when I was sitting on my mom's shoulders. "They're not as bright when you're on level ground. You know, now that I'm thinking about it, I can hardly remember what the stars look like. I haven't gone to see them since…"

A bitter taste crossed my tongue. I swallowed it down.

"Since she died," I forced out. "Three years ago."

Polly's expression didn't waver. I looked at her and waited for her to break eye contact, the way people usually did, but she didn't. She just stared right back at me. And then all of a sudden we were just looking at each other. Funny how that worked.

"You know," I said. I tapped my fingers nervously against the table. "You'd think I'd get over it, but it's just... harder than I thought. I don't know. I just didn't know that she would leave behind such a..." My brow furrowed as I struggled to find the right words. "A big... a big... black hole inside of me."

Polly finally spoke.

"Drew Hartford," she said, "you are no black hole."

"Yeah," I said, a bit absently. "I know. I'm sure you get the picture."

Polly shook her head then, surprising me. "No," she said. "I don't get it. I don't really get it at all. I can't tell you I know how you're feeling because I don't. Nobody in the world does. And I would be lying if I told you I understood what you're going through, because I don't, and so there's nothing I can say that can possibly help you. For that, I'm sorry, because it sucks that I can't. I wish I could do more but I just *can't*."

Her honesty stunned me into silence. I thought back to how Brent's parents offered their help, but it didn't mean anything. Now here she was, telling me that there was absolutely nothing she could do, and it meant so much more than anything anyone else could ever have told me.

She told me the truth. No little white lies, no *I'm here if you want to talk*, no *I know how you feel*, none of those senseless promises. I'd be lying if I said it didn't hurt, because it did. It did hurt. Nobody *wants* to hear that they're alone in their grief, that no one could understand what they were feeling inside.

I didn't want to hear it, but I desperately needed to.

"But I'm sticking by you, okay?" Polly said. She reached out and touched my arm. "Even when you want to get rid of me, I'm gonna be right next to you and I won't budge an inch. Because I like being next to you. That's the truth."

How could I ever want to get rid of her? I stared at her, trying to burn her image into my memory forever. I never wanted to forget how she looked in that moment. "Yeah?"

"Yeah."

We made our way into the movie theater together and bought a large popcorn at the concession stand. Every time our hands met in the bucket, I swear I felt static crackling up the sleeve of my wrist.

The film was awful. It had to have used every possible cliché in the book. The romance was cheesy and paper thin, the characters were all shallow and flat, and the plot was ridiculous, barely cohesive.

But as we sat in that dimly-lit movie theater, Polly hooted with laughter, gasped in shock at every plot twist, and cried true tears at the climax. I'd never seen anyone react to a screen like that, with so much raw, honest emotion. So despite it all, I was so happy to be walking out of the theater next to her.

"That has got to be the best movie I've ever seen," Polly told me as we walked out into the night. She turned to face me, stopping in her tracks. "Did you like it?"

She had the biggest smile I'd ever seen on a person. "Yeah," I said. "It was good."

Polly's smile softened. Didn't fade away, just mellowed out.

"You don't have to lie, you know," she said.

"What?"

"I could tell you didn't like dinner. Or the movie."

I jutted out my chin. "I don't know what you're talking about."

Polly held my gaze for a moment. And then she laughed. She threw her head back and just laughed and laughed.

"You can just say you didn't have fun," she told me. "My feelings won't be hurt."

"Okay." I raised my hands. "So I didn't like the food or the movie."

"Ha!"

"But I *did* have fun. I'm not lying when I say that."

Now Polly's smile dropped. Her eyes went wide. "You did?"

"Polly," I said. "I'm always having fun when I'm with you."

Polly was stunned. She didn't say anything for a few moments.

Then she grinned.

"You're funny," she said.

She reached over and took my hand. This time she laced her fingers through mine. She'd held my hand before, but never like this. Never with our fingers entwined.

There was such a difference between those two ways of holding hands. Clasping palms was soft and comforting, but it wasn't intimate the way lacing fingers was. You could let go whenever you wanted. When you laced fingers with someone, you attached yourself to them, stuck onto one another and made it fit in all the tiny corners somehow; and even when you let your hand relax, you were never really letting go.

The little bursts of static I'd felt back in the theater were gone. No, that was no static I was feeling.

The very blood in my veins turned to lightning.

And we walked home just like that.

28

All of my nerves were still buzzing with electricity when I got back home. It was late. I closed the door after myself, a faint grin playing at my lips.

The smile died instantly when I walked into the kitchen, where Dad was sitting with the lights on dim. I stopped dead in my tracks in front of him.

I looked at him. He looked at me. Neither of us moved.

"So," Dad said. "You told me you were going to the movies with Brent."

I tried desperately not to roll my eyes. I heaved a sigh. "He bailed last minute," I said. "So I invited Polly instead."

"That's a pretty crafty lie," Dad remarked. "You know you bite the inside of your cheek when you lie, Drew. That's your tell."

"You noticed," I said. I turned to face him now. I wasn't smiling or pleased by it this time. I was just annoyed.

"I always notice," Dad said.

It took all of my willpower not to bark out a laugh. "Okay," I said breezily. "Alright. I'm going to bed, Dad." I started to turn towards the staircase.

"No, you don't." Dad crossed his arms. "We're not done talking here."

I stopped. I let out a breath I didn't know I'd been holding, then turned slowly back around on my heel.

"So," Dad said. "Are there any other things you've been lying about?"

I made a conscious effort not to bite my cheek. "No."

"Really," Dad said. "I didn't even know Polly existed, Drew, and all of a sudden she shows up on our doorstep saying you two have this— this special bond, you two are super close— why didn't you tell me about her, Drew? Why aren't you telling me these things?"

"I was going to," I said, only half-meaning it. "It never seemed like a good time."

238

Dad's lips pulled into a frown. "You're too grown up for me now," he said. "Is that it? You can handle everything on your own? You don't need me anymore?"

"Okay, you're putting words in my mouth," I said, angry now. "You know what? I don't even know why you're acting like you cared. If Polly didn't show up today you never would have found out about her."

"I do care," Dad tried to put in. "Drew, of course I care."

"That's not true," I spat. "Don't act like you know my *tells* when—when you don't even know *me*, Dad, alright? You don't even know me. We're like complete strangers. So stop pretending like we're not, because you didn't care before so it's not fair for you to act like you care now!"

My mouth instantly snapped shut, my heart racing with adrenaline. There it was again. That bloodthirsty demon that lived somewhere deep down inside of me, which I'd tried to subdue, but had already lashed out at Polly— and now it was here on full display once more. I shoved it back down as quickly as I could, but there was no undoing the damage.

Dad was staring at me, too stunned by the outburst to respond. He blinked a few times, trying to recollect himself. His brow furrowed, his frown deepening. "Drew—"

"Sorry," I said quickly, slipping right back into default submission. "Sorry. I didn't... I don't know where that came from." *I knew exactly where it came from.* "I didn't mean any of that." *I meant every word.* "I'm just tired, that's all. Can I please just go to bed? I just want to sleep."

Dad cleared his throat awkwardly. "Yeah, yeah, sure," he said dismissively. "That's fine."

"Okay." I swallowed. "Um, goodnight."

"Goodnight."

I turned back to the staircase and went to my bedroom, shutting the door. As soon as I was alone, I collapsed onto my bed, covering my face with my arms.

I became dimly aware of a sort of sickly sweet scent, like a perfume that had gone stale from sitting out too long. Lifting my head, I glanced to the side, where the boutonniere from winter formal was still sitting on my desk.

I'd completely forgotten about it. Now that I was looking at it for the first time since the dance, I realized that the edges were wilted and brown, tainting the once pure, satin white of the orchids. The petals were shriveled and drooping, the leaves fallen and lying discarded on the desk.

Something hurt deep inside of me, aching painfully, but I had no idea where it was or how to fix it. I slammed my fist into my pillow, buried my face in it, let awful sobbing sounds escape my mouth, but tears never came.

What's wrong with me? I couldn't figure myself out, couldn't understand what the horrible feelings were. None of it made sense to me. I was miserable inside and out, rotted all the way through. I kept trying to cover all of it up with Polly. Polly, my refuge, my shelter, my safety. But then I was always alone at the end of the day, and I was broken and beaten as I always had been.

I held my pillow up against my face until it began to suffocate me. My breathing slowly grew more and more labored. Then I couldn't breathe at all anymore. My lungs began to scream. When black started to creep in the corners of my vision, I finally pulled the pillow away, allowing myself fresh air.

You coward, said a voice in the back of my head. *This is your problem.*

Shut up.

You're always too scared to actually do it. You're always hiding.

I threw the pillow away at my feet. I hugged my arms close to myself, falling back down against my mattress.

You're always lying.

I closed my eyes, squeezing them shut tight.

I waited for tears to come. They never did.

29

Mrs. Pruitt ended the next Literature Society meeting the same exact way as the last one— "I'll see you all at our next meeting. Have a great day, everyone" — except this time she followed it up by saying, "Mr. Hartford?"

Everyone else was packing up and leaving. I crossed the room to her desk.

"Is something wrong?"

She smiled up at me. "No, nothing's wrong. You're not in any trouble. I was just wondering if you had a moment to talk."

I glanced back at Polly. She slung her bag over her shoulder.

"See you tomorrow," she called to me. There was a strange look on her face.

I turned back to Mrs. Pruitt. "Sure," I said. I sat down in the desk across from her and put my backpack down.

"I read your narrative," Mrs. Pruitt told me. "Now, I already knew you were a very gifted writer from your essays, but I think you have a real talent, Mr. Hartford."

I hadn't been expecting that. "Thank you," I said dumbly.

"You know, there are schools that give scholarships out for aspiring writers."

I chuckled politely. "I'm not an aspiring writer."

Mrs. Pruitt just raised her eyebrows at me. "Ms. Park told me you've got quite a passion for writing and literature."

I *really* hadn't been expecting that.

"Oh," I said faintly.

Mrs. Pruitt smiled. "I think you have a shot at winning one of these scholarships," she told me. "I have a list of competitions and prompts that you can take and look over—"

"No thank you," I blurted.

Mrs. Pruitt was surprised. She blinked.

"Um," I said, "I mean, thank you… but I'm not planning on doing any writing after high school. I'm going to study math."

"Oh," Mrs. Pruitt said. Disappointment was dripping from her tone. "Well, that's fine. Will you at least consider it?"

"Sure," I said. I smiled. "I'll think about it. Have a good day."

Mrs. Pruitt smiled back at me. "You too," she called after me as I walked out of the classroom.

Scholarships. That was insane. Even if I wanted to enter, what would I do if I won a scholarship for writing? I couldn't do *writing* for a career.

Writing was too risky. It didn't matter whether I liked it or not. What could I possibly do with writing after college? Besides, I liked math. Math was a sure option, a pathway that was practically already paved for me. Math was success. Math was...

My stomach dropped into my shoes.

Mathletes!

I'd completely lost track of time. I sprinted to the multi-purpose room. My legs were aching with each stride.

I threw open the doors. Brent, Jess, and Wallace were all standing on the stage.

"Sorry," I blurted.

In the back of my mind, I was hoping they would react the way they did last month. I waited for them to start laughing at me, going, *We haven't even started, silly!*

Instead, Brent was glaring daggers at me as I approached them. "Where were you?" he demanded.

"Literature Society," I said, cringing inwardly, already anticipating the onslaught of hysteria. "I'm sorry. I lost track of time."

"You missed practice for *Literature Society?*" Brent ground out. I noticed that he was holding Jess's hand tightly in his own. "What were you doing there?"

"Talking to Mrs. Pruitt."

"About what?"

I shifted my feet nervously. "She thinks I should write essays for scholarship opportunities."

Brent barked out a laugh, though there wasn't any humor in it. "Right, okay."

I furrowed my brow. "I'm serious," I said. "She thinks I'm good at writing. And..."

Brent's face hardened. "And?"

I shrugged. "And I kinda like it."

He stared at me in disbelief. "Drew, you're kidding, right? You do know English is for dumb people?"

"What makes you say that?"

"Drew," Brent said. He was shaking his head condescendingly, like I was just too stupid to understand. "Anyone can do English. Only smart people can do math."

I realized how similar this sounded to what I told Polly when she first showed up in my class. Regardless of what Polly had insisted that day, I decided that I hated hearing this out loud. It *was* jerkish. "That's not true."

"Of course it is!" he shrilled. "How do you think you're gonna be successful reading books and writing poetry all day, Drew? You seriously think there's a market for that or something? People would kill to have your brain when it comes to crunching numbers, and you're over here wanting to go frolic in the daisies writing a bunch of stupid *words?*"

I bit down hard on the inside of my cheek. I fought back the urge to scream.

"Our first tournament is in two weeks," Brent said. "You can't afford to just *miss* practice."

I swallowed. "I know. I'm sorry. It won't happen again."

Brent shook his head. "It better not," he spat venomously. "Come on, Jess."

Jess gave me a look as the two passed by me. "See you next practice," she said.

Wallace stepped down from the stage now. He winced at me sympathetically.

"He's just stressed, that's all," Wallace said. "Don't worry about him, Drew."

249

"I know," I heard myself say.

Wallace's eyes were concerned. "Are you okay?"

I took a deep breath through my nose. Then I smiled at him.

"Of course," I said. "I'm okay."

30

Just when I thought he couldn't get worse, Brent showed up furious the next day.

"I can't believe it," he was rambling. "I can't even believe it."

"What?" Wallace piped up.

"*Jess,*" Brent shrilled. "She broke up with me."

He dropped his lunch tray onto the table and sat down hard, arms crossed over his chest. I found it strange that he seemed more annoyed than anything else. Weren't you supposed to be heartbroken after a breakup? Brent didn't seem *sad* at all. He was just angry. So angry, in fact, that I could practically see the steam rolling off his shoulders as he sat there.

I cleared my throat awkwardly. "Sorry," I said.

Brent raised a dismissive hand in the air. "I don't even care."

Wallace and I gave each other looks. We watched as Brent fumed silently for a couple seconds.

Then he erupted again. "She said I'm too dramatic," he whined. "I'm too *dramatic!* Can you believe it?"

We met him with complete silence. He shook his head, too preoccupied with himself to notice our reaction anyway.

"You know…" Brent suddenly looked up, snapping his fingers. "I bet you anything she got that idea from Polly."

Now I looked up too, narrowing my eyes. "What does Polly have anything to do with this?"

"She's always saying nasty stuff about people," Brent said. "That's all. She probably talked trash about me to Jess. Made me look bad."

"Or maybe Jess just happens to think you're dramatic," I bit back.

Brent shot me a look. "What's that supposed to mean?"

"I just think it's stupid to jump to conclusions like that. You're blaming Polly for something she had no part in, just because it's easy to pin the blame on her."

Brent rolled his eyes. "Oh, whatever," he said. "You're just being defensive over your little *girlfriend.*"

"She's not my girlfriend," I said.

And at the exact same time, Wallace said, "She's not his girlfriend."

I froze. I turned to Wallace.

"What?" I said.

Wallace blinked. "Polly's not your girlfriend," he said, without missing a beat.

"Who said that?"

He looked baffled. "You just said it too!"

"I know I did, but who told *you* that?" I demanded.

"Polly said it during class," Wallace told me. "She said you guys were—"

31

Just friends.

I didn't believe it.

Just friends.

No, no, that wasn't true. I knew it wasn't true. Wallace was wrong. Clearly he'd misheard something.

Just

friends.

No. It wasn't true. He was mistaken. Polly wouldn't say that about me. She wouldn't. He was wrong.

Just—

32

"You look kinda sick again," Polly said during class.

I was hardly listening to her. Wallace's words were still ringing through my ears. *Just friends.*

Part of me was screaming to just ask her about it. Surely this was all some big misunderstanding. *Just ask her.* But I was too scared of what she would say.

"...are you even listening to me?" Polly was poking my arm. "Drew."

I slowly blinked myself back to reality. It was like surfacing after floating miles and miles under the ocean. "Huh?"

"You're not gonna throw up on me, are you?" she joked.

"No." *Maybe.*

"You must have the weakest immune system on the entire planet." She reached out to feel my forehead for a fever. "Come here."

I pushed her hands away mindlessly. "I'm not sick," I assured her.

She watched my face for a few seconds, like she didn't quite believe me. She dropped it. "Did you hear anything I said?"

"Hm?"

"I was just saying I want to drive to the top of Sycamore Hill," she said. "Have you ever been there?"

"No."

"Then go with me. Tonight."

I looked at her. "What do you want to do there?" I asked.

"Surprise," she sang coyly. "Can you drive us?"

I looked at her. Didn't I already tell her I didn't like to drive? I couldn't even legally drive her places, not without my adult driver's license. And aside from that there was my whole crippling fear of driving.

Now, logically, any friend would just say 'no'.

But I was *not* just a friend. And I just didn't have a choice when it came to her.

So I said, "Yeah."

Polly smiled. "Cool."

"Cool."

My ears were ringing that whole day. I got myself dressed up for her once more. Same routine as last time. Did my hair. Wore yellow. Except this time my movements were all sluggish.

Dad was working. I wasn't even sure if he'd noticed that I'd come home. I figured he wouldn't notice I was gone for the night.

So I took his keys and went out into the driveway. The neighborhood was empty except for me.

I put my hand on the car door handle. It felt foreign under my touch. I pulled. It opened. I got into the car. Closed the door.

The seat was leather. I hardly remembered what it felt like sitting in the front seat of a car. The last time I'd been here was three years ago.

It's okay, I told myself. I took deep breaths in an attempt to steady myself. Nothing had changed about the car. Same mechanics as always. Same technique.

I put the keys into the ignition and felt the engine hum to life underneath me. My heartbeat quickened and I closed my eyes. I waited for my heart to slow back down before putting my foot on the gas pedal.

I pulled out of the driveway, my hands gripping so tightly around the wheel that my knuckles were beginning to turn white. I focused on my breathing. In. Out. In. Out. Everything's fine. You're not going to—

Don't think about it.

In.

Out.

My hands started to sweat. I wiped my palms on my jeans at stop lights. Focus, focus. *Don't* lose focus. Eyes on the road at all times. In. Out.

I hardly even registered the fact that I'd made it to Polly's house until she opened the passenger's door.

I started a bit, every nerve in my body on edge. She slid into the seat next to me and I forced myself to calm down.

"Hi," she said. She was wearing a long dress that went down to her ankles. She had a cardigan wrapped up in her lap.

"Hi," I said.

I put the car in reverse and got us back onto the road. I was surprised that I'd gotten to her house without a single hitch. I let myself relax a little, leaning back in my chair. Everything was fine after all.

"I like your shirt," she said. She grinned. "You've been wearing a lot of yellow lately, haven't you?"

"I guess I have."

"All to impress *me?*" she cooed.

I smiled half-heartedly at her, but I didn't say anything back. My eyes were fixed on the road.

She sat back in her chair. We were silent for a few more minutes. Just driving. Driving.

"Did you know," Polly said conversationally, "that they make lemon-scented pencils?"

I was focusing on turning the car. Deep breath… focus…

Polly examined the beds of her fingernails. "I saw them at the store the other day," she went on. "Crazy, right? I can't believe the book fair didn't have any."

I hummed in acknowledgement. Polly waited for me to respond. I still didn't say anything.

"They didn't smell like lemons, though," she said. "Just smelled like vomit again."

Silence.

Polly turned around in her car seat to face me now. "Hey," she said.

"Hm?"

"What's wrong with you? You've been acting weird all day."

I shook my head. "Nothing's wrong."

I looked back at the road. I could see Sycamore Hill approaching in the distance. I let myself breathe. We'd made it with no hitches.

Polly narrowed her eyes. "You know, you always say that, but I don't think you mean it."

"I'm fine."

She was frowning. "You could at least *look* at me."

I sighed, exasperated. Then I turned to look at her.

"I'm *okay*," I told her.

And then, out of the corner of my vision, headlights veered into the road.

My eyes widened. I turned back to the road frantically to see a car swerving towards us in the dark.

I seized the wheel and yanked it the opposite direction so hard that the wheels skidded under us. Beside me, Polly was yelling something that I couldn't hear. We

261

skidded and turned, spinning, the world outside becoming a blur.

The car never came to a stop for some reason. My head was still spinning, still spinning. Headlights were burning into my eyeballs. Piercing. Aching. I couldn't see straight.

My breaths were coming in short gasps, like they were being raked out of me. It was like I'd forgotten how to breathe entirely. My lungs were screaming for air and I couldn't figure out how to get it to them.

Lights were dancing before my vision, a million multi-colored headlights that turned into sirens flashing. They were all screaming and wailing in agony. Cars were flying across the street, crashing and burning and exploding. Smoke filled my lungs, crawling down my throat and spreading thick across my airway, suffocating me.

The sirens turned into beeping. Unsteady. *Beep. Beep.* A long one. Then a short one. And then

there was a long one
that never
ended.
Flatlined.
We lost the patient.
No. No. No.
Mom was lying on the white mattress, her
eyes closed. Cars crashing in the sky, hitting
trees, hitting rocks, hitting each other. Cars
crashing and people dying and stars falling
down and down.

I looked at Mom but suddenly it wasn't
Mom anymore. Suddenly it was me lying
there and I was flatlining.

Did you even know that you were dying?

My heart monitor was dead. Fire was
eating up the sides of my bed. The heat was
intense, sweltering, my skin blistering and
bubbling and melting down to the bone.
Mind-numbing pain took over my senses,
leaving me a mess of charred, raw flesh and
screaming welts.

But you did, didn't you?

Breathe. Breathe. No, I couldn't. Not with the smoke. Not when I was burning and dying and falling, falling forever.

Shut up. Don't think about it. Don't talk about it. Pretend it never happened because it never happened it didn't shut up shut up shut up.

You knew and you just pretended you weren't.

Breathe. Breathe—

"Breathe!"

My eyes flew open. I gasped for air, finally managing to find it somehow. My lungs sighed in relief as air rushed in, and my body started to work again.

I slowly blinked myself back to reality, wheezing quietly. Polly wasn't sitting next to me anymore. She was outside the car, standing beside me and leaning over with the car door open all the way.

"Breathe," she said again. "We're fine. We didn't crash."

I took a long, painful gasp of air and looked down at myself. I wasn't dead. I was

264

just sitting in the front seat of the car, and my seatbelt felt too tight all of a sudden, almost suffocating.

I fumbled with the seatbelt. My fingers weren't working properly. They'd gone completely numb. "Get this off me," I said, my voice garbled. I hardly even recognized myself.

Polly gently took my hands in hers and pried them off of the seatbelt. It was only then that I realized my hands were trembling. No, not just my hands— my entire body was shaking like mad.

She undid my seatbelt. I nearly tumbled out of the car. She grabbed my shoulders as I stumbled out, steadying me, keeping me upright.

"I need—" I was choking. "I need to sit down—"

"Okay," she said quickly. Her eyes were wide. She must've been scared. I couldn't blame her. "Come here."

She guided me to the sidewalk. I collapsed, sitting hard on the pavement. It took all of my willpower not to fall over into the grass on the other side.

"What was *that?*" Polly asked as I caught my breath.

"My—" I coughed. "My mom."

"What?"

I closed my eyes. "Car crash," I managed to say. "She died in a car crash."

Polly had fallen silent. When I opened my eyes again, she was staring at me.

"Jesus," she said. "Why didn't you *say* anything?"

I swallowed hard. Shook my head. "I'm—"

"I swear to god, if you say 'I'm okay' one more time, I'm going to gouge my eyes out with a spoon."

I choked out a weak laugh even though it hurt my sides.

She wasn't laughing. "Why did you do this?" she asked quietly.

"Do what?"

"Drive." She was looking at me with her black eyes. "You didn't have to drive us here. You do know that, right? You didn't have to."

I took a deep, shaky breath.

"I'd do anything for you," I said.

Polly shook her head. "No."

I blinked. "What?"

"You'd do anything to yourself," she told me. "You know, you're always acting like everything's fine, like you don't care about anything, like you're okay. And for the longest time I thought it was because you didn't know about yourself. But that's not true. Your problem isn't that you don't know the truth, it's that you don't *like* the truth."

I said nothing. I was too stunned to say anything.

"Remember, a long time ago, when I asked you what you see when you look at yourself in the mirror?" Polly said. "I thought you didn't know. But I get it now. You know what you see. You just don't like it."

I did know what I saw. My eyes stung. "Stop," I said. "Stop talking, Polly."

"So you know it's true," she kept pressing. "Then what's the real reason you came here, Drew? Why would you do this to yourself?"

"Because I—" I sucked in a breath. "God, because I like you, Polly."

Polly recoiled like she'd been slapped. Her eyes were wide.

"I really *like* you," I said again, my voice flat and pathetic. It sounded almost like a plea. The words tasted bitter in my mouth as I said them.

Her face fell. She stared at me for a long moment, silent.

I waited desperately for her to say something. Anything. And then finally, her lips parted.

"Oh," she said.

And that's all it took. I knew it was over.

"Listen, Drew," she was saying. "I like you too. Just… not in that way. Like, at all."

There was no letting me down easy. She just said it like a slap in the face, shocking and painful. I reeled back from the impact, eyes wide, turning to face her.

"That's it?" I said, my voice shaky and incredulous.

Polly hardly even looked pensive. She shrugged, careless. She'd never been more cruel. "Yeah, that's it."

I sucked in a breath. My heart was shattering into a million different pieces all at once. I shook my head. My eyes were glued to my feet.

"Hey," she said. She poked me in the arm the way she always did. "Hey. Don't be upset. Come on. We're just—"

"Don't finish that sentence," I said. "Don't even finish that sentence."

She ignored me. "We're friends."

"We're not just *friends!*" I was practically shouting. She startled at how loud my voice was. "Polly, ever since you got here I've been falling in love with you. Don't tell me we're

269

just friends. If we're just friends, then why did you say you liked me? Why did you say I was cute? Why did you— why did you bring me to your house and show me your lemon tree and sneak me into the book fair and ask me to winter formal and hold my hand with our fingers laced and— and why on earth did you slow dance with me? Huh? If we're *just friends*, Polly, then why did you do that?!"

Polly was staring at me.

"Because I wanted to," she said.

Everything inside of me sank all at once.

"I did those things with you because I wanted to," Polly repeated. "I don't regret any of it, you know. I meant every second. I wasn't lying, Drew. I like you because you're my friend."

She took my hand in hers. My hands weren't numb anymore. I felt everything. Her fingers were soft and she laced them through mine once more, as she had done that night we went to the movies.

"You're my best friend," she said. "My best friend in the entire universe."

I stared down at her hand in my own.

"Yeah," I said. "You always say whatever you want."

"I know a lot of people don't like that about me," Polly said. She looked at me. "It's not that I don't care about anyone's feelings, or that I'm rude, or anything like that... maybe I am. I don't know. But I care about my own feelings too. I don't want to pretend to feel something just because other people expect me to. I don't like lying to anyone, especially not myself."

"I know," I said.

And I realized that I was smiling, for reasons I couldn't quite place. But I couldn't stop. I was smiling and it wasn't one of my polite smiles. It was a real one.

"You never faked anything for a second."

Polly squeezed my hand. We sat in silence for a few moments. Crickets sang quietly in the night.

"You wanna know why I brought you here?" she whispered.

She unfolded her cardigan. A pair of binoculars was in her lap.

"I've never gone stargazing before," Polly said. "I didn't have a telescope or anything, but I just brought these..."

I laughed. I took the binoculars from her.

"They're perfect," I told her.

She smiled at me. "I heard you can see every single star from the top of the hill," she said.

"Really?"

"Mm-hmm." Polly stood up. She was still holding my hand. "Let's go see."

She pulled me to my feet. I followed her up the hill into the starry sky.

As I was climbing up the hill it didn't feel like I was going up at all. It just felt like I was falling.

33

She was right, by the way.

We did see every star. Every single one. They were shining so bright in the sky that I can still see them now when I close my eyes, burning beneath my eyelids.

She showed me all the stars I never even knew existed.

And I was still falling, still falling, but surrounded by a billion twinkling lights.

34

The other team was faster.

It didn't matter how difficult the problems were. Every single time, the other team buzzed in before us. The match wasn't even close. Brent and Jess hadn't so much as looked at each other since they'd broken up, which didn't help our teamwork much. We'd only been going for thirty minutes when they called it.

The multi-purpose room was never full when we had Mathletes tournaments. Tonight was no exception. The few people in the opposing crowd stood up in their seats and cheered.

We'd never gone down like this before. We had losses in the past, but never this bad, and never this early on in the tournament. This was our first match. That meant we were out for the rest of the year. We didn't even place. It was *bad.*

Brent was the first to storm off stage wordlessly. The rest of us watched him go.

Jess rolled her eyes. "Probably just gone off to throw a hissy fit," she commented. "Per usual."

"Good job," Wallace said. He and Jess high-fived. Then he came over and high-fived me too. "Good job, Drew."

"I'll go check on Brent," I said. "See how he's doing."

"See you tomorrow," Wallace said.

"See you," Jess called.

I waved to them before turning and leaving the auditorium. It was cold outside. The ground was wet, even though I didn't know it'd been raining.

Brent was sitting on the curb in the parking lot. I approached him cautiously, my hands in the pockets of my Mathletes jacket.

"Hi," I called out.

He didn't look at me.

"Good job," I said. "We did our best."

I stood next to him. He looked up, glaring at me.

"That was not our *best*," he said. "*That* was humiliating. We got creamed. We didn't score a single point."

I pursed my lips. "There's always next year," I said, trying to sound hopeful.

It didn't work. Brent's brow furrowed in frustration.

"You don't care about this at all," he said accusingly. "I wanted to win *this* year, Drew. But apparently that doesn't mean anything to you."

I was taken aback. "Of course I care."

"Well, not like I do, okay?!" Brent stood up suddenly. He turned on me, furious. "You know, *maybe* if you showed up to practice and actually took this seriously, we would've won tonight!"

I stared at him in total disbelief. "So this is my fault, basically?"

"I'm just *saying*," Brent spat. "You're just always doing other things now. Like, writing,

Drew? *Writing?* Since when did you care about that? It just seems awfully convenient that right when you started hanging out with Polly, you bailed at my party, you missed practice, and now you think you want to do *writing?* Wake up, Drew! You're not a freaking writer! You're wasting your time!"

"No," I said firmly. "You know what? You are the *only* thing that's been wasting my time, Brent. *You.*"

Brent blinked in shock. Then he glowered. "Polly's been getting in your ear, hasn't she? That's why you've been acting all psycho."

"No!" I yelled. I was so loud that Brent's mouth snapped shut in surprise. "This isn't about Polly, or Jess, or *anyone.* This is about me and you."

"And what's that?"

"You're a bad friend!" I shouted. "You treat me like garbage! And you know, for the longest time, I just *let* you. That was my fault. But I'm done now."

Brent tried to cut in. "Drew—"

"No, this is the part where you *shut up and let me talk for once,*" I said. "You're always being a jerk to me. You used me to flirt with Jess and got mad when I left. I walked to your house in the rain just to apologize to you and then got sick for a week. Because of *you!* All you do is use me and blame me and walk all over me and I'm tired of it. I'm not your doormat, Brent. I'm not a tool or some toy for you to play with whenever you feel like it. I'm a real person and I've got feelings too, even if I had to deny them to accommodate you. And you know what?"

I peeled off my Mathletes jacket.

"I'm done with Mathletes, too," I told him. "I'm done pretending. I'm done pretending I'm okay with you bullying me and pretending I'm okay with doing math for the rest of my life. You know what? Maybe you're right. Maybe I'm not a writer. Maybe I'm wasting my time and maybe I'm stupid and maybe I'm gonna be unsuccessful and broke forever. But I love writing, and that's

278

more than I can say about math. So I'm done faking it, alright? I quit. I'm *done.*"

I threw the jacket down on the ground. It landed in a dirty puddle at my feet. All that expensive leather covered in grime. Brent stared at it.

The two of us stood there in silence for a moment, facing each other as I caught my breath. Finally I just turned on my heel and walked away, leaving Brent standing there with my abandoned jacket lying on the ground beside him. Alone.

I could feel my eyes stinging as I walked home. My nose was beginning to run but I just sniffled and ignored it. Stupid allergies. That was all it was.

Because I didn't cry, obviously.

I was still sniffing when I walked in my front door. Dad was sitting on the couch in the living room. He stood up when he saw me.

"Drew?" he said.

I ignored him. I kicked off my damp shoes and tossed them aside, storming past the room.

"Drew," Dad called after me. "Hey, what's wrong?"

"Nothing."

I kept walking.

Dad watched me. "Are you okay?"

"I'm okay," I said, my voice cracking.

I stopped dead in my tracks.

I turned back around. Looked at him in the dark.

And there were tears coming down my face.

And, yeah.

I was crying.

"I, uh." I wiped at the tears, but more took their place. "Actually, Dad, I'm not okay."

Dad's brow furrowed. "Drew," he said softly.

"I'm not okay," I croaked again. "I mean, I haven't been okay ever since Mom died, you know. I know I always tell you I'm fine and

280

not to worry about me but those were all lies. I thought that if I lied, maybe it wouldn't be as painful. But I was wrong. I was just pretending it didn't hurt. Pretending doesn't… it doesn't make things better. It just makes you numb. I kept telling myself that was fine, but it's not. I just want to feel again. God, I just want to feel like myself again."

Dad stood up from the couch. His eyes were sad.

"And—" I sucked in a breath that turned into a hiccup. "And I *know* that you have your own problems, I know you're busy with work and I know you're sad and you're broken but— but I am too. And I really, *really* just need you to be my dad right now. Please."

I tentatively took a step towards him.

"Um," I said in a small voice. "Can you hug me?"

And then he did.

His strong arms were wrapping around me and holding my back and I fell forward into him with a choked off sob. He hugged me and for the first time in years there was no distance between us at all. It was just him holding me in the living room, the same way he did when I was a kid.

I always thought that Mom had left empty space in our house, that she'd taken all the warmth with her when she'd gone. Now, standing there and hugging Dad, I realized we were the ones who'd built up all that space between us.

But just as we'd fallen apart, we came together again. I closed my eyes and let myself cry in Dad's arms. Like he was just my dad and I just was his kid. Because he was, and we were, forever.

Mom was still gone. That was how people were. They left you when you needed them most. They came when you expected them least. We loved each other. We hurt each other. We had each other. How could you not be content with that?

We stood there for what seemed like an eternity. I finally pulled back. My tears were soaked into his sleeve.

"I got your shirt all gross," I told him.

"Yeah, I know," he said.

He hugged me again and I was smiling with tears falling down my cheeks like stars in the night.

35

Wallace sat next to me at lunch, like
always.

Brent, on the other hand, was absent. I had
a feeling Wallace knew what happened
between Brent and I. He didn't say anything
about it, though.

"My parents were really upset about the
tournament," he laughed to me. "Like, more
upset than I was. They were devastated."

"Really?"

"Yeah." Wallace drummed his fingers
against the table. "They were going nuts.
Stress eating and everything. Like, 'how
could you not make it past the first round?
The *first round?*'"

We both erupted into laughter.

"It *was* pretty sad," I said.

"Yeah," Wallace agreed. "I mean, someone
has to get out first, right?"

"Yeah."

We quieted for a moment.

Then Wallace said quietly, "I'm going to come out to my parents."

I looked at him. "Really?" He nodded. "Dude, that's amazing."

"You know," Wallace said thoughtfully, "I kept telling myself that they would be upset. That, I don't know, maybe they wouldn't accept me. But you know what I realized?" He gestured at himself. "I'm the only one holding me back. I was the one who couldn't accept myself. But I'm better now. I'm... really happy with myself, you know? And I think they will be, too."

I stared at Wallace in astonishment. Then I grabbed him by the shoulder and pulled him close to me, hugging him tightly.

"Oh," he squeaked faintly. "This is new."

"I'm really proud of you," I told him. When I pulled away to look at his face, I saw that he looked almost like a new person. I realized that he wasn't different at all— this was who he was his whole life. He was just clearer now, more confident, a little brighter.

285

"Thanks," he said. His cheeks were pink from all the praise.

Then he looked up. Suddenly his eyes were fixed on something else.

I followed his gaze, looking behind myself. I found myself face-to-face with Brent.

"Hey," Brent said nervously.

"Hey," I said.

Brent anxiously tapped his foot up and down. His hands were hidden behind his back. "Um," he said. "Well, I know you kinda hate me right now, and you know, I don't blame you or anything—"

"I don't hate you."

He boggled. Then cleared his throat, regaining his composure.

"Oh. Um. That's— that's good." He swallowed. "I just wanted to say that you were right. I was... I mean, I've been a total jerk to you. That wasn't cool, and you're right, I haven't been a good friend. But you are a really, really good friend, so... I hope you can forgive me."

Before I could say anything, Brent pulled a folded up square of cloth from behind his back. He held it out to me.

"Take this," he blurted.

I took it. I unfolded it. It was my Mathletes jacket that I'd thrown into the street last night, except it was completely clean. And here was a new patch sewn on, with three new letters in red: *MVP*. Brent started talking again.

"Nora's on the team now," he said. "I could've just given her your jacket, but, well... I know you're done with Mathletes and everything, but I just wanted you to keep this. It's— it's yours, after all, whether or not you're on the team. You know?"

I stared at the jacket. Traced my finger over the red patch.

Then he added, "I sewed that on myself. Isn't that romantic?"

"You did?"

"Yeah. I did. So, are we cool?"

287

I pretended to be deep in thought for a few seconds. Then I said, "You still haven't apologized."

Brent let himself grin now. "Drew Hartford," he proclaimed dramatically, "from the bottom of my heart, I'm sorry."

"And from the bottom of *mine*," I said, "I forgive you. We're cool."

"Cool."

I smiled. "Yeah, cool."

36

We moved seats in English.

I was crestfallen. It felt like the end of an era for some reason. I found myself sitting next to Sara Dean. Polly was sitting a thousand miles away in the other corner of the classroom, with Connor Brightfield.

Everything felt different now. My days with Polly seemed to have come to an end.

During class, I snuck a glance at her. I found that she was already looking at me, almost like she'd been waiting for me to look at her.

We locked eyes.

She stuck her tongue out at me from across the room.

Maybe some things were different, but not everything.

I stayed behind after class. Went up to Mrs. Pruitt.

"Hi," I said.

"Mr. Hartford," she greeted me. "How can I help you?"

"I've been thinking," I told her. "Like you asked me to. And about that scholarship list you've got… do you think I could take a look at it?"

Her eyes lit up. "Of course," she said. She fumbled through her files for a few seconds before finding it. Then she handed it to me. "Here you go."

"Thanks." I folded it and slid it neatly into my backpack.

"So," Mrs. Pruitt said. "You're deciding to give writing a chance after all. What's changed?"

I glanced over at my old desk, where Polly and I's old seats were empty. *Everything.*

"I guess I just decided that I really do like writing," I said.

But then I realized I'd used that word again. *Like.* And it was still as much of an understatement as ever.

"I love writing," I corrected myself. "I really, really love writing. I think it just took me a while to finally accept that I do."

She leaned forward in her desk.

"Well, I'm glad to hear that you do. Good luck," she told me. "You're going to do amazing things."

As soon as I walked out of her classroom, a voice was waiting for me by my side.

"Hey," it said next to my ear.

I leapt back. "Oh my *god.*" Polly was snickering outside the doorway. "How long were you standing there?"

"Long enough to overhear that you finally came to your senses," Polly told me. Then she poked me in the arm. "Mr. *Smart English.*"

"Well, someone helped me realize I was being very stupid."

"Very *very* stupid." Polly smiled. "Sitting next to Connor for the rest of the year is going to be so boring."

"Yeah?"

"Yeah." She put on a new voice, one I hadn't heard before. "Who's going to enjoy my Randle Patrick McMurphy when we start reading *One Flew Over the Cuckoo's Nest?*"

I was awestruck. "What kind of accent was that?"

"Welsh. Duh."

"McMurphy's Irish."

"Oh, don't worry, that can be arranged." Polly grabbed my hand. "But later, okay? Right now I want to show you something. Come with me."

Well, yeah. Of course I went with her.

It's just like I said. I didn't have a choice when I was with her.

Polly and I walked until we reached her neighborhood and we were back at her little brown house. I waited for her on the driveway while she went inside.

"Close your eyes," she ordered. "And don't even think about opening them until I say so."

So I closed my eyes. I heard her slide her keys into her front door. I could picture the little meerkat dangling from the keyhole as she stepped inside the house. There was silence for a minute. And then I heard her footsteps again, then the door closing.

"Open," she said.

I opened my eyes. Polly was standing in front of me, holding two glasses of lemonade. She held one out to me.

"No way," I said. "Is this…?"

"Homemade," she sang. I took the glass from her; it was cool under my fingertips. "Drink."

She watched me over the rim of her own cup as I took a sip. I was surprised by how sweet it was. I thought it would be really sour, made of pure lemon juice and no artificial flavoring at all, but it tasted almost exactly like store bought lemonade.

"This is really good," I told her.

"Thanks," she said. "And it's *au naturel.*"

Suddenly I remembered something. "Your boutonniere," I blurted before I could stop myself.

Polly looked at me, narrowing her eyes in confusion. "What?"

"The boutonniere you made," I said, "for winter formal... um, it died." I struggled to meet her gaze, feeling guilty.

But she wasn't upset. In fact, she guffawed at me, a hysterical grin lighting up her face. "Yeah, okay, and?"

I was stunned by her dismissive reaction, her easygoing laughter. "And— well, they were orchids, weren't they? I thought you loved your orchids."

"I do love my orchids," Polly agreed. "But, Drew, they're *flowers*. That's just how it works, you know? You cut them, they die, and they grow again."

I found myself thinking about those stars once more. This whole time, I had been thinking about how they were falling and how they were dying. I had never once thought about how they were being born just the same. New ones in new places, even if they didn't twinkle just as bright, or in the same patterns as before. They were still there, alive and burning.

We both sipped her lemonade in silence for a while. I stared into the bottom of my glass. Then I stole a glimpse at her over the rim of my cup, and I realized—

I couldn't get myself to fall out of love with her no matter how hard I tried. Not really. I was trying to, but then I realized that I was never going to stop. She was a part of me forever. I'd tried to figure her out, tried to pin her down, but she just flew away every time. Flying and dancing and frowning and smiling and everything in between.

I loved everything about her. I loved that she didn't hide and I loved that she didn't pretend. I loved that she said things that hurt so badly without a care in the world, like she hardly seemed to notice she was killing you inside. I loved that when she did say the nice things, they were real and true and made you feel like you were looking down on all the rest of the world in a throne of clouds and sky.

Polly Park was the girl who had broken my heart into a million tiny pieces that night on Sycamore Hill. But she was picking up every single shard of my heart and putting them back, except they were slightly out of place now. They didn't quite fit together the way they used to. It was different now. Whole again, but different.

People don't really take well to change around here.

I recalled telling her that at the book fair in a far-off, honey-colored haze. There was no way for me to make sense of her, but I also knew that things around here had changed ever since she came along. Polly had completely flipped the world upside down. Everyone was a little different now because of her. I was a little different now, because of her.

296

She was kind of teaching me how to feel again.

I was still falling in love with her and I didn't know if I would ever stop. I didn't know if I wanted to.

"What're you thinking about?" Polly asked quietly next to me.

"You," I said truthfully. "The night on the hill."

"Did it hurt?" she said. "When I said all those things to you?"

I nodded. My eyes were glued to hers. I couldn't look away.

"I'm sorry that it hurt you," she told me, "but I'm not sorry that I said it."

"I know."

Polly's hand found mine. Our fingers intertwined, like lightning once more. Her voice dropped low and she said, "Can I tell you something, Drew Hartford?"

"Anything."

"I lied."

That caught me off guard. I looked at her curiously. I never thought I'd hear those two words coming out of her mouth. I must have misheard her.

"What?" I said.

"I lied," she said again. Something secretive lit up behind her eyes then. "You wanna know the real reason why the lemonade is so good?"

"Yeah?"

Polly glanced around, almost like she was nervous someone would overhear despite the fact that we were standing alone on her street. Then she leaned in close to my ear.

"I used preservatives," she whispered.

I burst out laughing. She grinned, watching me absolutely lose it next to her, laughing so hard that I almost dropped my glass.

"What's so funny?" she asked, feigning ignorance.

I shook my head.

"You really are incredible," I told her.

She smiled. I smiled back.

298

And I can tell you that standing there on that empty street with her hand clasped tightly in mine, her name on my mind and the taste of lemons on my tongue, I was very happy. Very very happy.

And that— *that* is the truth.

Megan Dang is a 15-year-old writer. She has a passion for storytelling in all forms and spends her free time writing books, screenplays, and webcomics. Another one of her hobbies is art, so she was very excited to illustrate her first book cover for *What We See While We're Falling*. More of her artwork is featured on her Instagram, @meg.ikarp.

Made in the USA
Coppell, TX
25 September 2020